Joseph Parrish Thompson

The Sergeant's Memorial

Joseph Parrish Thompson

The Sergeant's Memorial

ISBN/EAN: 9783337092689

Printed in Europe, USA, Canada, Australia, Japan

Cover: Foto ©Raphael Reischuk / pixelio.de

More available books at **www.hansebooks.com**

Your aff son
John H. Story

THE

SERGEANT'S MEMORIAL.

BY

HIS FATHER.

NEW YORK:

ANSON D. F. RANDOLPH,

No. 683 BROADWAY.

1863.

New York, April 15, 1863.

Rev. J. P. Thompson, D. D.,

Dear Sir :—Fully recognizing the paternal privilege of preserving in your own heart's sanctuary the memory of a child whose life and death have been alike happy and honorable, and appreciating also your natural unwillingness to compile for publication the facts and circumstances which made the last months of your son SERGEANT JOHN H. THOMPSON *so precious, still, permit us, on behalf of the young men of your Church, to suggest that as he gave himself and his life to his country, his countrymen, his comrades, young men all through the land, for their own profit and encouragement in this dark hour of their country's history, have a right to know and perpetuate those principles which prompted him to go forth to die, "having on the whole armor."*

May we not hope, also, that incorporated with the above there may be the record of some of those patri-

3

otic thoughts which his death aroused in your own heart and in the hearts of the many who knew him, and who mourn with you the loss his country has sustained?

Trusting you will be induced to accede to our request, and at your earliest convenience place the manuscript in our hands,

We remain,

In the bonds of Christian sympathy,

Yours truly,

HENRY C. HALL,
CHARLES BELL,
W. H. BRIDGMAN,
CHARLES T. RODGERS,
W. H. THOMSON,
HENRY K. WHITE,
F. B. LITTLLEJOHN,
J. A. McGEE,
GEO. G. HALL,
E. N. RANNY,
AMBROSE LEONARD,

WM. A. JENNINGS,
A. JENNINGS,
R. W. HASKINS,
CHARLES L. HALL,
W. D. MOORE,
WILLIAM E. GAVIT,
JOSEPH H. WHITEHEAD,
FRED. M. ROBINSON,
AUSTIN ABBOTT,
CHAS. S. SMITH,
L. M. BATES.

32 *West Thirty-Sixth Street, May 22, 1863.*

My Dear Friends:—In consequence of my absence from the city, your kind letter of the 15th ult. has but just now come into my hands. It meets me upon my return from a visit to my son's regiment, where I found his memory as fresh and tender as on the day when his comrades delivered to me his dear remains.

" He did not aspire to distinction," said an officer; " he was only anxious to serve his country. He was too modest for a soldier, too modest for anything in this world." How, then, can I accede to your request, and unveil that gentle, retiring life?

" Every one of us," said a tent-mate, " has some little memento of the Sergeant;—we thought so much of him; and if you could send us his picture, or some sketch of his life, we should prize it so much!" And when I find this spontaneous request of his comrades in arms seconded by the spontaneous request of

(5)

my own "*Young Men's Bible Class,*" many of whom knew him as a brother in Christ, how can I withhold from his country the memory of one who, while he sought nothing for himself, gave all he had to her cause?

And so, at once doubting and trusting, I place these fragmentary thoughts and memoirs at your disposal. Your grateful Pastor,

JOSEPH P. THOMPSON.

Messrs. HENRY C. HALL,
      CHARLES BELL, and others.

THE

SERGEANT'S MEMORIAL.

I.

* * * * It was Sabbath evening. I had preached to young men upon purity of life and a true faith in Christ as the highest manliness and the best qualification for serving their country and mankind. As I left the church, a friend inquired of 'the army boy;' and this had led to pleasant talk of one who early learned to follow whatever was pure and lovely and of good report. Just at the time of rest came a violent ring, and a telegram. My heart read it before it was opened; but those few hurried words—
"Your son is dangerously ill—come at once,"
—awoke every energy of fear, hope, love. In an instant I had started, only to learn that no train would leave till morning. He there, in Virginia, in tent or cabin, sick,

weary, dying, and I not able to move toward him for hours, when every moment was
an hour, and every hour a day, and a day
was a life. Hemmed in by the impossible!
Nay—shut up to Him who, like a Father,
pitieth his children.

My heart told me he was already dead.
Why then should I be so impatient to reach
him? Did not my heart bury him when it
said Go? Yet by the first and fastest train
I was on my way—whither?—to what?

Again detained in Baltimore, my heart
now said, "he is *not* dead—I will procure a
furlough; or if not this, will convey him to
the best hospital; or if not this, will watch
by his side; I will take with me provision
for every comfort, against any emergency;
I will send for the home physician; the
freest and the best must be for the boy
who has given everything for me, for his
country;"—the click of the telegraph in the
hotel office said, "Your son died this morning." Died this morning? Yet though all
is over, I cannot wait for the train to-mor-

row : the express to-night will, *must* stop, and leave me by the road-side near his camp.

As I enter the train, the sentinel with loaded musket and fixed bayonet, challenges me for the inspection of pass and baggage. The car is filled with soldiers. As we move on, there are guards at every bridge, at every station ; I am within the seat of war. It is far past midnight when we reach Harper's Ferry ; through the gloom I look unconsciously for *his* camp as it was last summer, and for the greeting of surprise he gave me then. We are at Martinsburg ; it is but ten days since he left here, and his last letter described the heavy, weary march, through mud and snow. Those picket fires under the open sky—how many nights has he paced thus, watching through storm and cold !

The train slackens; it is for me ; I barely jump to the ground, when the living rush on their course, leaving me to seek the dead ;—alone, in the dark, where the sentry is pacing to challenge me, where all is

strange, and gloomy, and desolate. No—
not all strange ; some one speaks my own
name ; "I am Captain Paine ;" a friendly
arm leads me to the house ; a friendly voice,
not without emotion, tells me of the last
scene. I go up into the little chamber
where two soldiers are watching their dead.
Tenderly and reverently they uncover the
face :—IT IS MY FIRST BORN!

II.

HE was my first born.   Twenty years ago he came to bless my early manhood in the spring-time of my ministry; to open within me a strange new life that seemed another self, that was to be my imitative self, my counterpart self, and by-and-by my posthumous self.   What hope enters into a man, what love goes out from him, when he thus begins to live in his first-born son! Heir to no affluence, family, fame, he was heir to Liberty through the blood of Puritan and Covenanter mingling with the martyr-blood of the Revolution, and heir through many generations to the covenanted grace of God.*

* John Hanson Thompson was born at New Haven, Conn., September 3, 1842.   His earliest ancestor in this country was

2   (13)

At the time of his baptism, one of the first theologians of the land was my guest. I asked him—"if his parents are sincere and faithful, if faith is strong and teaching

John Thompson, one of the first settlers of Stratford, Conn., who came over from London in 1635. A well-preserved family tradition relates that he came out at first to see the country, and soon returned to England to make arrangements for a permanent removal. To reach his home, he had to diverge from the main road and to go some miles afoot. A farmer upon the route, learning that he was from America, detained him to take a meal and to give the news. Thompson described the new country as full of savage beasts and savage men; but added, with a tone of exultation, that he should go back, notwithstanding, for there one could worship God according to his conscience. "Is that indeed so? Would that I were there," exclaimed *Mirable*, one of three buxom daughters at the table. "But, could you," asked Thompson, "for the sake of Christ, endure the trials and perils of that wild and far-off country?" "Yes, gladly, by God's help," answered Mirable. This young Puritan maiden had not long before been publicly exposed in the pillory for attending a Separatist conventicle. When John Thompson returned to New England, Mirable came also, as his wife; of whom was *Ambrose* (1652), of whom was *John* (1680), of whom was *John* (1717), of whom was *William* (1742), of whom was *Joseph* (1769), of whom was *Isaac*, yet living, of whom was *Joseph Parrish*, of whom was *John Hanson*. This *Hanson* represents a family of Covenanters, my maternal ancestors, driven from Scotland to the North of Ireland by the storm of persecution.

William Thompson, above (born 1742), was a Lieutenant under General Wooster's command, and fell at Ridgefield, Conn., April 27, 1777, "bravely fighting for the liberties of his country." He was buried at Stratford, and his tombstone records that "he lived greatly beloved, and died universally lamented."

true, is there any reason why this child should not, from his first moral consciousness, be God's willing holy child?" I received no light then; though my friend thinks he has found it in the theory of a preexistent state of probation and fall. This I know, and this the boy came to know and acknowledge — that he did not grow up without sin, and that the way into the kingdom was through renewal and sanctifying grace. Yet this also I know, and will testify, that from infancy he was so gentle and pure, so conscientious and sincere, so loving and true, that he gave large hope of early piety to those who watched his training; and these qualities, like his very features, grew only the more marked in the same mould, as he grew in years. It was a household saying, that "Johnny was never known to deceive;" and no member of the family can recall any unpleasant passage or incident in his home-life. Very precious is the memory of that life;—too precious to be here unveiled.

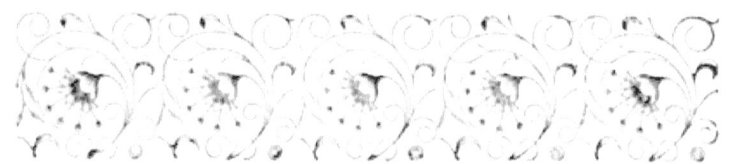

III.

SOME rough winds blew upon that young
life, some dark clouds gathered about it,
and clinging to his father with the strength
and the gentleness of an unquestioning
faith, the boy of nine crossed the sea to find
new homes in England, France, Italy. The
pet of the sailors—climbing fearlessly into
the topmast, and running over the rigging
like a squirrel,—the pet of the cabin—
making his merry laugh chase away the in-
ertia of sea-life; now pacing the quarter-
deck in the captain's watch, now sighting the
compass for the man at the wheel, now with
Jack in the forecastle, now trolling his line
astern, now on the lookout for whales or ice-
bergs,—how the child baffled the sea, and

(16)

made even sickness and fears brighten into health and hope! Then it was that his soul became a part of mine.

"What a little gentleman he was," say the good American friends who gave him his first home in England; "so kind, so polite, so tidy, so merry, so obliging. How we all loved him!" And a dear English lady, who welcomed him almost with a love of adoption, and who has since tasted the bitterness of parting with her first born, writes, "I look back at his face as I knew it, almost too sweet and patient-looking for a child, and then at the picture of him in his regimental great-coat, with his sword by his side, and realize with tears and sorrow all you have lost! Rather one should say, lost *sight* of, for it is not lost, but gone before."*

For months in Paris, in the family of my dear friend, Rev. Leon Pilatte,† forgetting his English with Mademoiselle, learning the

---

* Mrs. Joseph Warne, of Oxford.

† Mr. Pilatte is now pastor of a Waldensian church at Nice, France.

games of French children in the Luxem-
bourg, and the wonders of nature in the Jar-
din des Plantes; then for other months at
Mentone, in Italy, learning to swim, in the
Mediterranean, and to climb upon the mari-
time Alps; counting bread and olives better
than the richest dairies of America, and the
costume of the simple villagers better than
the pageantry of Hyde Park; how many
lessons of man, of society, of life, did his
young heart receive for future moulding, all
under the guiding hand of that religious
household in which the piety of France and
of America were so happily blended. For
nearly a year he knew no other home.

"He was a boy," writes Mrs. P., "I would
have given as a model to my own children;
and how often have I regretted that my
own little boys have not known him, es
pecially now that my eldest (ten, last December), just the age he was when with us,
so often makes me think of him. Dear
Johnny's picture of Mentone is very truth-
ful. 'Those were happy days I spent there!'

he says, and we say so too, adding that he himself stands out in bright colors among our reminiscences of Mentone, with his bright eyes and beaming face—a face I cannot well forget.

"I think John was an extraordinary child. He possessed those qualities which in childhood or manhood are rightly called noble; such as unselfishness, courageousness, deference to the opinions of others in spite of an independent and reflecting mind; and he seemed to try to cultivate these qualities conscientiously.

"He was very forward to oblige, and it seems to me I can almost hear now, his glad 'may I, may I,' so frequently heard, when any little service was called for. During our journey from Paris to Mentone, this was particularly observable. As children generally are, he was in great glee about the journey we were going to make, and talked much of all he would do and undertake; and if any difficulty arose, seemed to think he could remove it at once, by all he would

take upon himself. In addition to a knapsack which he had begged to consider as his
own property, he would have loaded himself
with the bags and cushions of the whole
party.

"He was a conscientious boy. There
was no disregard of obligation, or careless-
ness about duty in him, that I ever perceived. He did his duty without troubling
others to look after him to see that he did
it. He applied himself diligently to the
study of the French language, and boldly
essayed the conversational department, in
which he made rapid progress. I remember
his asking me once, what day of the month
it was, in a phrase which was quite new to
me; and I can see his bright face with a
suppressed smile upon it, peering over the
balustrade, as he was going up stairs, as he
said—'*quel quantième est-ce?*'

"There is another incident that we recall,
which showed his courageous resolution
Mr. Pilatte had arrived late from a journey,
and being hungry, we soon spread a supper-

table for him ; but there was no water, and
our fountain, the nearest place where we
could obtain fresh water, was at a good and
lonely distance from the house. I suppose
the servant must have gone to town for the
night, as she did sometimes, for I remember
that the cry was raised—'who will go and
fetch some water?' A silence ensued, while
each one recollected that there was no water
in the house, and that to have any, some one
must go a good way in the dark. Johnny
was the first one to break the pause. ' I'll
go,' said he, and seizing the pitcher, he soon
brought it back full, and he himself full of
pleasure with the little sacrifice it had cost
him to slake the thirst of our weary traveler.

"I do not recollect but one instance of
his having required reproof at our hands.
It was for having beaten the dog. That
love of power inherent in man, and almost
always manifested at an early age, thus
showed itself in him toward poor doggy,
who was thrashed for nothing at all ; but we
never had occasion to repeat the reproof."

Either "doggy" deserved the thrashing, or this act of injustice was expiated in after years by the fond and ready patronage of the whole species. Even in his tent-photograph the little pet dog appears nestling in his blanket and sharing his rations.

With this affection for animals I recall the general artlessness of his tastes. The boy had seen the treasures of London and Paris, had witnessed the pomp of the burial of the Duke of Wellington and of the proclamation of Louis Napoleon as Emperor; had heard of the marvels of Rome, Naples, and Constantinople;—but when on leaving him in Paris, I asked what present I should bring him from the East, he gave me this little slip of paper that now lies before me — folded, sealed, and inscribed, "To be opened when you come in sight of Mt. Sinai."

Paris, Dec. 6th, 1852.

DEAR FATHER :—I suppose that you are now in sight of Mt. Sinai, and you know that you promised me you would get me some sand for an hour-glass when you were in the desert; but I would rather have it from Mt. Sinai, if you can get it there; but don't get more thàn a bushel. I told you that I would give you a letter of introduction [to Mt. Sinai], and is not this one?

Your son,   JOHNNY.

I fulfilled the commission. He had the wished-for hour-glass. It lies beside me now—broken in the middle, its sands prematurely run out.

IV.

THE boy loved flowers; not with a mere childish wonder and delight in their growth and their blooming, but with an intelligent, care-taking interest in their structure and their properties, their names, beauties and varieties. Symptoms of ill-health, that threatened to become chronic,—the residuum of scarlet fever and measles—demanded a thorough change of regimen; and an agricultural school in Cornwall, Conn., afforded the desired opportunity for the cultivation of rural tastes, with a regular but moderated intellectual training.

Boating and swimming in summer, coasting and skating in winter, log-splitting, spading, plowing, all that pertains to garden and farm work and to the athletic sports of the country, tended to give robustness to his constitution, and finally conquered the infirmity that threatened to be the bane of his life. At thirteen he has his garden patch of melons, corn, tomatoes, etc., competing for the school premium with all the zest of a member of the American Institute. But in the cultivation of flowers he exhibits a taste that grows into affection.

"Did you get the copy of the *Homestead* that I sent you, with my composition about flowers? Please keep it for me, as it is the first thing I ever wrote that was printed. Have you read a book called 'Hiawatha,' by Longfellow?" The printed composition, were it at hand, might have an interest now that did not attach to it at the time; but the taste that it indicated matured with years, diffused its delicate fragrance throughout the house, gave zest to many a ramble through the woods, and even relieved the roughness of camp-life by levying upon nature for such leafy and floral contribu-

tions as could be found, to ornament the
tent. Not a book or a paper in his tiny
knapsack library but contains some remnant
of gathered flowers. He had learned to
name and to classify all trees of the wood
and flowers of the field, all grains and
grasses and growths, long before most city
lads can distinguish the contents of a grass-
plot border.

As he himself delighted to watch some
choice flower, to analyze its parts, and to
preserve its outline and impression when its
substance had faded, so it is a joy to go
back in thought and watch the unfolding of
traits that grew to be fragrant and precious
virtues, and the first outlines of which are
preserved in these boyish letters ; to note
his careful precision about matters of fact—
as when his brother is written to, post haste,
to examine " whether the New Haven cars
have tongues on them, when drawn by
horses," and is charged " to be sure that he
understands it, as it is a case of great importance ;" to note his punctuality in writ-

ing home, and his care in sending particular messages to every member of the family ; to note his appreciation of brave and manly qualities, as when he pours out his boyish enthusiasm for Dr. Kane, after reading both his expeditions, and laments that he could not have seen him before his death ; to note the kindling of noble impulses for liberty, as when he stands up alone in the school for Fremont as the freemen's candidate, and denounces the outrage upon Senator Sumner, in an "exhibition" speech ; to note his care of his clothing, and his economy in his little possessions, as when he puts his new knife away, because he has not yet lost or used up the one sent him in the first part of the term ; to note his detestation of vice and crime, as when he recounts the profaneness and the deceptions of schoolmates, or writes an indignant comment upon "the awful wickedness of New York," as reported in the newspapers ; to note his considerateness with regard to his parents' wishes, in every wish or plan of his own, and his loving deference of address ; to note his grateful appreciation of his school-boy privileges : " I keep up my French, and will try and get my Latin as well as I can. The more I study it, the more I like it ; but still I do not see what good it will do me . . . . . I am glad you think I am improving in my studies, because I try all I can to learn, while I have so good an opportunity ;"—to note, especially, the flower of love that so beautifully unfolds itself in this greeting to the newly-born : "As to *home*, although I am away from home, I have not forgotten what it is to have one. I am very glad to hear that I have got a little baby brother, and he shall never repent that I am his brother, nor say that I ever treated him unkindly, if I can help it ; and there is nothing I should like better than to be able to do something for him sometime."

V.

BEAUTIFUL was the love that bound together the eldest and the youngest of the household, for the six years from that day of greeting to the day of parting. The school-boy found no more delightful pastime in vacation than to entertain for hours " the baby brother "—teaching him all childish games and sports, and, as his mind opened, all pleasant things about flowers, birds and animals, such as children love to hear. In the summer recess, it was a day's delight for John to take Willie on a ramble through the woods for wild-flowers, or hunting squirrels, or to build chip boats for the perilous navigation of the brook. No higher society seemed so kindred to his gentle, loving nature as this little confiding brother, who would go with him anywhere, everywhere, and live in his own light.

Fragments of toys that had baffled parental patience and ingenuity, would be gravely laid aside till Johnny should come home, with the most implicit confidence that his skill would restore them. And so it did. Nothing in the line of such inventions ever surpassed his powers of contrivance, and not the most hopeless breakage could discourage his patience. In the soul-union of these two, Faith walked unquestioning and satisfied by the side of Love.

When the school-boy had entered college, and began to know the fellowships of maturer life and the aspirations of manly pride, there was "still nothing he liked better than to be able to do something for the baby-brother at home ;"—to send him a flower, to paint him a picture, to make some new contrivance for his amusement when away ;— and at home to take him to museums, parks and fountains. And when the college youth became a soldier, he would sit down after guard or picket duty, and print in large letters for childish eyes, some little adventure with explanatory sketches.

What love could be sweeter, purer than this of a young man, a college student, an army officer, for a little child? When the child looked upon his elder brother in the last sleep, with a strange awe of the mystery of death, his young heart told how faithfully Johnny had fulfilled the promise of the first greeting. When a few days after, John's captain, on furlough, called at the door, his first exclamation was, "Ah! this is Johnny's little brother that he always talked of; every body in camp knows Willie."

VI.

A HEART so gentle and so loving, so pure and simple in its tastes, so noble in its aspirations, needed the Highest and the Best to satisfy its longings ;—needed that fellowship with the pure, the good, the true, which is found only in God manifest in the flesh. The more pure and lovely the character that engages our affections, the less can those affections satisfy the soul they would encircle as its home. The more one rises above the common level of character, the more does he need "to know HIM that is true, and to be in Him that is true, even in his Son Jesus Christ." Were one sinless, but mortal, he would yet have need of Christ ;— Christ's spiritual illumination,

Christ's gentle sympathy, Christ's guiding wisdom, Christ's sustaining love. Much more is Christ's redeeming, renewing, sanctifying grace a necessity for those who are sinful as well as mortal.

A judgment more delicate and penetrating than mine, an eye more constant and watchful than mine, a love more sympathetic than mine with childish experiences, and more sensitive than mine to manifestations of Christ, had ventured to pronounce this child a child of God in his ninth year, when an angel-brother opened the gates of heaven to his wondering eyes. Theories of a metaphysical conversion held my eyes doubting! But the day of manifestation came.

"Dear Mother," he writes, "I shall be so glad to get home once more; at least five years of my fourteen have been spent away from home! But it must be just as you and father think; you know best. Everybody here is very kind to me, yet I am real *home-sick;* I mean it; I never was so before; I am so lonely; nobody to talk to that I can

tell everything I want to ; it is hard for me
to study ; hard to seem cheerful."

With a view to a more systematic preparation for college, he had been transferred
from his farm-school to a grammar-school at
Cambridgeport, Mass., and he missed of
course the out-door life and the hearty
recreations of his loved " Cream Hill." But
his mind was also thrown back upon itself ;
and he found and felt that "aching void"
which is often the first consciousness of
higher spiritual needs.

" I know, dear father" he writes at fifteen,
"that the culture of the heart is of very
great importance, and I often think that I
should become a Christian without any more
delay. I try to do what is right, and I pray
to God to help me, to give me a new heart,
and to teach me how to love and serve Him.
I think of these things more sometimes than
at others.

"I was invited to attend the young men's
prayer meeting a few weeks ago. I have
been twice, and I like to go very much.

I hope it will do me good. I think I know what your wishes are on this subject, and I will try to follow them as well as I can. I showed your letter to uncle E——, and he talked to me about it very kindly." He is approaching the moment of transition into the true life of the soul;—the seeds of holy faith and love long germinating in his heart are about to flower.

His letters now are filled with reports of Bible-class lessons, of sermons and religious themes that had awakened his attention, and that indicate the working of his mind. But religious thought and prayers, and "trying to do right," are not enough to bring the sense of peace with God. To a soul made conscious of its sins and its needs, peace and joy can come but through one medium; and in that blessed spring-time they so came to him.

"My dear father and mother, rejoice with me, for I hope and trust that last night I gave my heart to Jesus. Oh, how much better I feel! Uncle E. told me that no one could do it for me ; so, before I went to bed, I trust I gave my heart to Jesus.

" I must go to Boston, to-morrow, to give my testimony in this cause. Oh, pray for me that I may keep on."

The date of this letter (March, 1858) refers it to a season of unusual religious sympathy in Boston, of which Park Street Church was for a time the centre ; and the allusion to " bearing testimony in Boston " is explained, a few days later, in a more particular account of his decision to serve Christ.

"I do wonder that I have not done this before, because it was so easy when I once determined to do it. In the vestry of Park Street Church I first promised to seek the Lord ; promised a stranger. I do not wonder that I have not done this before, because my heart was so wicked." Thus the contrariety and the conflict of experiences described by Paul in the seventh chapter of his epistle to the Romans, the good and the evil, the ready-willing and the not-doing, reproduce themselves in this child-heart, until the favoring moment of decision comes, and Christ, received in his all-sufficient strength and grace, animates the soul both to will and to do. To come to Christ is so easy, when the heart is determined upon it, that the wonder always is that it was not done before ; yet the heart is so full of evil that the wonder still remains that it was ever done at all.

Upon how small an incident the salvation of a soul may turn! Reading in a newspaper some report of the religious meetings in Park street, the school-boy took his weekly half holiday for a walk into town, to observe one for himself. A stranger remarking his serious interest, gave the prompting word, and the great decision of life was there resolved upon. Happily, he had the guidance of a sympathizing friend and a judicious counselor, in the uncle whose house was his home. The new life developed itself less in the way of outward demonstration, whether of word or action, than through the quiet manifestation of Christian principle and love.

4

"John's state of mind," writes his uncle, a month later, "has interested me much, as far as I have been able to draw it out. He does not express himself very fully, nor manifest much emotion. I see nothing inconsistent with the hope he indulges, while his uniform quiet, steady habits do not afford much opportunity for the exhibition of marked religious experience. He inquires with new interest about religious truth, expresses confidence in his hope, and penitence for sin, and looks upon prayer meetings very differently from formerly. He is thrown very little into company, and probably does not feel drawn into personal effort to reach others. He has once or twice spoken in the young men's meeting, of his purpose and hope."

At the same time, John's own letters give such glimpses of his new experience as make me feel now, as I felt at the time, how thorough and genuine, and also how characteristic it was.

"I cannot talk or write about religious

feelings at all times, father; did you not find it so? It is hard for me to express my thoughts on paper."

"Oh! how kind God has been to let me live on so long, while I sinned against him. He is merciful and slow to anger."

"I know, father, that you would like, of all things, to have me become one of God's ministers, and give all my powers for his service. But I would rather talk than write about that; and I must think more before I decide,—if it is for *me* to decide."

"It is a very pleasant thought to me that I have so many friends in heaven, and that if I live in the fear of the Lord I shall soon meet them there."

"One verse gave me a stronger determination to be very watchful over my actions and thoughts. I am surrounded by temptations to do wrong in many little things; but I pray much for God's Holy Spirit to deliver me from them. Pray for me, as I know you do."

Some months after, moved solely by his

own desire, he publicly confessed Christ,
by uniting with the Broadway Tabernacle
Church,—in whose fellowship he continued
until death, and from whose sanctuary he
was borne to the grave. One who was a
deacon of that church in 1858, and who had
much opportunity to know John, volunteers
this reminiscence. "I well remember the
incidents attending his conversion. I remember his appearance before the Committee of the Church;—how well satisfied I
was that he was sincere, that he had weighed
the import of the act, that he knew what he
was doing, though in the modesty and sincerity of his heart he said but little. I met
him several times afterwards, and never
without thinking, 'here is a young man
wholly devoid of the frivolities of youth, and
who is living *for a purpose.*' But little did
I think he would so soon accomplish his
destined work on earth. I have often
thought, if I should live to see it, what station of usefulness he might fill. It never
occurred to me that his sun would set in the

early morning. How beautiful to see the young and ardent heart consecrated to Christ! And how sublime to see the same heart, with all its high aspirations in this life, consecrated to country;—after having counted the cost, yet saying, Here am I. And how heart-rending to think such costly sacrifices must be made to have a country!

"Every fiber of my heart beats in unison with the cause that the dear one gave his precious life to sustain. I honor his patriotism, his manly, his Christian decision. His memory will be ever dear to me. And should I live to see the day when I can say, 'My country, one and undivided,' I shall think of those who with brave and manly hearts, though perchance with tender and delicate frames, dared to offer up their lives to make it so."

4*

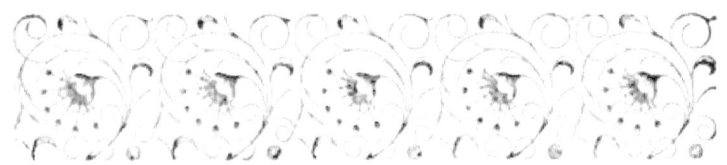

VII.

I COULD even be jealous of the homes
that so long divided him from mine, and
of the friends who now claim his memory as
a family treasure, were it not that he himself
always reserved that sacred word Home for
one household, and loved that with an affection not only undivided, but matured and
strengthened by the unavoidable separations
of years. But while he never could be
weaned from his proper home, he carried
into the several families—at Manchester, at
Mentone, at Cambridge, at New Haven—in
which he lived as a son, the same gentle,
cheerful, obliging disposition, the same careful and considerate habits, the same pure

and manly ways, the same helpful ingenuity, the same enthusiasm for the noble and the good, that made him even as a child the abiding comfort and joy of the house.

His ready fingers would construct an Æolian harp or an aquarium with equal ease; would dissect a sewing-machine at first sight, then put it together and claim the privilege of using it for himself; would acquire the complicated arts of prestigiation, and practice these for the bewilderment of little children, the amusement of the family circle, or the entertainment of a bedridden invalid; would prepare all manner of curious, ingenious, and beautiful things, for gifts and ornaments; mottoes and devices in skillful penmanship; sketches in crayon, ink, or color; picture frames in cones, leather, or passe-partout;—ah, this copy of Palmer's Faith that *he* framed, it leads me now with a deeper want and a more tender meaning to the Cross!

"We recall with pleasure," writes his Cambridge guardian, "our intimate acquaintance with him, and the intercourse we had with him while he was a member of our own household ; his correct life, his kindness to the children, his identification with our interests, his ingenuity and skill, and especially his hopeful experience of a change of heart."

That "kindness to children" prompts him on receiving a money present for his fifteenth birth-day, to consult whether he shall buy a squirrel, a canary, or some gold-fishes, for the pleasure of his little cousins, while he will gratify his own tastes by subscribing for the best agricultural journal.

Indeed he himself then edited, printed, and published a tiny journal of his own! The printing-press and type-case were of his own construction ; and I find among his later papers various diagrams for an improved power-press, apparently suggested by his youthful experience in typography.

One who has made boy-life a special study, and whose pen has enriched our juvenile literature with the model sketches of

"Robert Dawson" and "Reuben Kent," sends this reminiscence :

"I have a wee paper called the 'Weekly Wonder,' bearing the date, Feb. 22d, 1858, in which it says 'the editor intends to have a good time this week in Portsmouth.' He came and called upon me, and left me this, the fruit of a home printing-press experience, which I kept—expecting one day to show it to the grown-up editor, or minister, or lawyer. And this youthful editor was John—your dead yet living John! I took it out from my desk when I saw his death, and wondered if the tall and beautiful boy who gave me this were he! Ah, my dear friend, who can repair the terrible breach made in your family? God can make you willing to have it so ; as he made you willing to put him on the altar of sacrifice—but oh, the desolating sense of loss! I know they say, 'not lost, but gone before ;' yet it *is* loss ever while we live—a loss which the Father of our spirits and the God of grace and consolation makes up in spiritual gains and

promise, perhaps; but, after all, with the
sense of loss still aching, yearning. I feel
with you and for you.

"The account of John's last hours which
you sent to your friends was very affecting.
Precious is the evidence that 'all was right'
with him for the last great struggle.

"What a re-affirmation are we having of
God's great law of vicarious sacrifice! Will
it not issue in such a peace as the world cannot give, neither take away? I believe it
will, and a glorious future is before the
country."*

Another lady friend, of rare discernment
and cultivation, who saw him in these blos-
soming days, gives this picture of his gentle
and winning conversation:

"When John was at school at Cambridgeport, his aunt brought him over to see us
one afternoon, and on another day he found
his way by himself. I thought and said
then that I had never seen a lad who impressed me as he did; in every way so

* Mrs. Helen C. Knight.

attractive and winning ; at an age generally considered an awkward one with boys, there was a grace and a modest dignity in his bearing, and an ease and frankness in his conversation, that surprised and delighted me. No one could see him without wishing the next time might come soon. We had, I remember, quite a long talk, partly playful and partly serious.—He went with me to a garden seat, where we had this pleasant conversation under the trees. If he had been like others of his age, it would not have so dwelt in my memory, but I have never forgotten it or him ; and if Mrs. G. seemed to me an aunt to be envied because she could have him with her, and if in that brief interview I could recognize something noble and unusual in his nature—a purity, refinement and rare gentleness—how inexpressibly dear he must have been to you who thoroughly knew him, and how inestimable your loss in his early removal. Still his father must feel that the consolation is in proportion to the immensity of his loss.

To have owned him, called him *his*,—to have trained him to such admirable excellence, to have given him first to his country, and then in his unstained, un-sullied youth to his God and to heaven, where the angels were waiting and wanting him—oh, what happiness in it all, in the midst of deepest grief ; a strange joy and fervent gratitude to God for the gift of twenty years, for the blessing of his life and of his death !"

VIII.

WAS it predestined that the boy should be a soldier? A country life still fascinated him, and the pursuits of agriculture, to be ennobled by science, seemed for a time to fill his aspirations. In this vein he has "a little plan to propose" for a summer recess. "I soon will have a vacation of seven weeks, right in the midst of haying time. Why could I not work a part of the time— a month, perhaps—on some farm near where you will be, and earn something? It will make me strong, and I would feel more like study during the winter. I have determined to ask you about it, and if you and father think well of it, why, I am ready to try it." So he hired himself out for the

haying season, and the farmer reported that
he well earned his board and wages.

He tried in every way to endure hard-
ness ; and, notwithstanding a rapid growth
in stature, he succeeded by gymnastic exercises and robust occupations, in gaining a
well-proportioned muscular development.
But this was best accomplished by means of
the military drill to which he was subjected
for two years, at Dr. Russell's Collegiate
and Commercial Institute, in New Haven.
His hankering after an agricultural rather
than a professional life, and my own doubt
of his ability to endure the confinement of
professional studies and labor, had led to his
transfer from a course preparatory for college to a mixed classical and scientific course,
with a view to a general education.

"I use the military drill," said Dr. R.,
"as an auxiliary. It promotes discipline ;
it forms habits of punctuality, order, and
obedience ; it gives physical culture ; it furnishes a vent for boyish vivacity ; and, beside, it gives young men such a knowledge

of tactics, that they will be able to handle a
musket to good purpose, in any emergency."
In those days this last consideration was of
least account. Yet, then and thus it was
that he acquired the knowledge of arms
which, at the outbreak of the war, gave him
the assurance that he could serve his country to advantage, and which, in a raw regiment of volunteers, made him, as his colonel
testified, " worth more to his company, than
any man in it."

Our education of children—whatever plan
may be involved in it—is determined at
each step by the expediency of the hour.
But underlying all our measures, controlling
all our plans even in their fluctuations, is
the far-seeing, far-reaching plan of the Infinite Father, shaping his instrument for his
own end.

But, muscular development and military
drill, were not pursued to the neglect of
mental and moral culture. "Acting and
thinking," is his chosen motto, for success in
life, " throwing *all* one's powers upon the

one thing to be done." And here is the day-
dream of that halcyon time. "For ten
years I must work; then a traveler's life
until I know foreign lands. Returning, I
will build my house; fill its libraries, gal-
leries, etc., with the results of my travels;
join scientific societies; study, read, write,
and publish till the end! But for this I
must work now; so, here goes for Whately's
Reasoning, and Chambers' Zoölogy."

— But what a treasure of substantial re-
alities comes to light in this book of school-
boy compositions, dating at sixteen. Not
that they exhibit maturity of thought, or
extent of reading,—for the fragmentary
character of his education had not favored
either rapid or symmetrical development,—
but they show a regard for moral culture,
which made him beloved and even respected
beyond his years. "What constitutes a
gentleman?" he asks; and his answer enu-
merates honesty, truthfulness, kindness, or
true politeness, "that will not suffer us to
insult or injure, in any way, by word or

action, those whom fortune has not favored
as much as ourselves ;" neatness, punctuality, for, " if a person is behindhand in meeting his engagements, it is a sign of bad
training, and ill-manners ;" and then he
adds : "above everything else, every one
should have the love of God in his heart ;
and if he strives to serve Him, in all things,
he will be a gentleman indeed."

Concerning " reputation," he writes : "we
are all making our reputations now ; every
word and action will tell in future. Strive,
then, to gain a good reputation ; you need
not be a great orator, commander, or writer,
to gain it, but be honest, be diligent, generous and kind. Make yourself respected
and loved by your teachers and schoolmates ;
for your reputation at school will follow you
all your life."

A subject had been assigned for composition, under the title of " the advantages and
disadvantages of telling the truth." He
opens his essay with the remark : " I think
that the wording of this subject is rather

5*

unfortunate, for we should have it decided once for all, that it is always best to tell the truth, and never best to tell a lie. . . . . If a man is justified in lying to save his life, a child is justified in lying to save himself from a whipping,—and we should have fine society if children were thus brought up! . . . The Bible should be our guide in this matter ; and how can any one think it disadvantageous to tell the truth concerning anything, to save life or reputation, to please or displease, to make money or friends, or to accomplish any purpose, when we read in that true book, 'all liars shall have their part in the lake that burns with fire.' "

Writing of " manliness in school-life," he makes it essential to this, that there should be habits of industry, of politeness, of truth, of honor—" an honest and upright course, and obedience to rules ;"—and this he urges, because " the habits formed in school, will always follow us," and because " all the qualities of manliness are right and proper in the sight of God."

In an essay on "learning to take care of ourselves," he sums up all by saying, "form the habit of thinking clearly and rapidly, of knowing when you are right, and then going ahead."

And, finally, in answering the question, "for whom and for what am I working," he, says : "Am I working for myself alone? Ought I to be working for self, alone? No : to work for self, thinking of no others, is simply selfishness. If then, I work not for myself alone, whom do I work for? Is there not One, above all others, whose I am, and for whom I am to work? Yes; and in His holy Word I find this command : 'Whether ye eat or drink, or whatsoever ye do, do all to the glory of God.' Is not this a glorious thought, that I am working, not for myself, nor friends, only; but for that great Being who made me, and who gives me all I have? In all that I do,—study work, or play,—I am improving or abusing the talents He has given me; and in proportion as I improve them, so shall my re-

ward be. Thus it seems that I am working
for my Heavenly Father, and that He is the
Being for whom and for whose glory all
should work."

IX.

DID ever a boy regard Latin as other than a senseless imposition upon his time and talents? Did ever a boy grow up to the stature of a college examination without questioning the wisdom of his seniors at divers steps of the preparatory course? This boy at least was no exception. And this was the point and the only point, at which his will came into opposition with parental wishes, but always to yield with a manly grace.

At fourteen, he says, " I am getting along very well in all my studies except Latin, and that I do not make much progress in, because I do not understand it nor like it at all. I think I might just as well spend

the time on something which will do me
more good when I get older as on that
which does not seem to pay for the time I
spend on it."

At fifteen he has gravely argued the question of College with his uncle,—and has
settled it in the negative. "Uncle E. just
asked me what I was studying for. I said
I did not know.

"'Are you going to college?'

"'No, sir. I guess and hope not.'

"'Why, what do you dread?—hard
study?'

"'I don't dread anything; but I do not
wish to go.'"

Still, his whim, or prejudice, or fancy, or
whatever is the cause of this temporary
aversion to a college course, never takes the
form of obstinacy; and so a word of coun-
sel from home brings the response, "I was
glad to get your kind letter. I think that
within a year or two I shall be able to decide better about my employment than I can
now, so I will not ask any more questions,

if I can help it;"—and this also; "I am trying to learn all I can at school, and at all other places; for I shall never again have so good an opportunity."

His reported standing in every school, and the volunteer testimony of teachers, show that it was never study, as such, that was irksome, but only the thought of a long prescribed course whose practical bearing upon the pleasure or the usefulness of his future, he was not yet in a position to comprehend. The conflict between a desire for the best results of education and a distaste for the preliminary routine, breaks forth now and then, in such strains as this: " On Thursday evening I went to hear —— ; the best lecture I ever heard. How he must feel to hold such an audience in close attention for over two hours. I would sooner have his place than that of the Prince of Wales; for what comparison is there between a crowd drawn by a man's rank and name, and one drawn and moved by a man's eloquence?

"Of course you will say, why don't you go to college, then?—which is just my trouble, for I have no inclination for college but quite the reverse."

I had compromised upon this ;—that if he would master Latin, the first step toward a liberal education in any department, the question of entering college should be reserved for his own maturer judgment ; and having graduated creditably at Dr. Russell's Institute—venting his patriotism withal in a prize declamation upon the battle of Bunker Hill—he entered the scientific school of Yale College in the fall of 1860, intending to pursue the regular course in that department. A little experience in the attempt to master physical science without a broad intellectual culture, satisfied him of his mistake, and awoke in him the very decision that the advice of others had failed to secure.

Writing of engineering, he says, "I see plainly that this is not the life for me. I should not be happy in it ; the thing is not

in me. I do not like a business, money-mak-
ing life. Mother, I will tell you plainly
that I would like best to be a minister, but
I *dare* not be, I cannot be."

One who has known what it was to review
a youthful profession of piety by a later
standard of intellectual measurement, and
to subject affections and emotions to the
analytic processes of the judgment, will sympathize with this dear boy in the honest and
testing struggle he now endured between a
heart that yet believed with trembling and
a reason that questioned his dearest faith
and hope. "When I joined the church," he
continues, "I firmly believed as I professed.
But I was ignorant of much,—and one should
never go on blindly thinking he has the Saviour when he has not."

It was but a passing cloud—enough of
darkness to make the Saviour's presence
more desired, and therefore the more felt
and prized when the soul, emerging from the
vacancy and terror of unbelief, realized that
He yet *was* there. And as this cloud of

6

doubt and despondency rolled away from
the inner spirit, there came a clearer light
upon the outer course. Why is it that his
new light makes my eyes so misty that I
can hardly transcribe the words in which he
announced it?

"Nov. 5, 1860. Dear Father, I sent a
long letter to mother to-day, which were
better unsent. I wrote it in desperation, for
I feel that I am *mistaken :—you* and my
friends are *right.* The course I am now in
is not the course I need.

"Uncle D., by chance, called here this
morning, and we fell into a long talk, in
which he gave me much good advice, and
has fairly talked me into college, so that
freely I own up wrong. and desire to make
up for all lost time. . . . . I have been a
fool, and it will serve me right, if you say,
'No ; keep on as you are.' . . . . Being very
sorry for the trouble I am giving you by my
former folly, I am, I trust, a wiser and certainly a repentant son."

Though hiding this great consolation in

my own heart, it was out of its blessed fullness that I preached, on the following Sabbath, from the words, "*I have no greater joy than to hear that my children walk in truth.*" I never again commended the ministry to his choice; but, on leaving Phillips' Academy for college, he told me playfully, that he liked his Andover quarters so well he had re-engaged them for three years succeeding his graduation at Yale.

It was not needed that the test of death should be added to this test of doubt, to reassure him that he had the Saviour. But since it was not given to any of his friends to see him die in the far-off camp, it is grateful to remember the foreshadowing of the triumph there that was given here, when in a sharp and critical disease he lay for days upon the very edge of the grave. As he grew better, he expressed his great anxiety for personal friends whom he thought to be unprepared for death and eternity; adding: "I have been thinking a great deal about ——, since I have been sick; I think that if it had pleased God to take away my life, I should have been ready. I have not felt at all afraid to die, because I believe that Christ has forgiven all my sins."

X.

WITH an energy and persistence that proved the thoroughness of his purpose, he began at once under a private tutor at New Haven, to pursue the Andover seniors, by forced marches, through the Anabasis; and having outmeasured their parasangs, he entered Phillips Academy, in December, 1860. Of course he entered at a disadvantage, from the irregularity of his classical training, and at first he felt this keenly. "I will do my best in my new position; but I shall have hard times, and if I fail, all will be lost." As the class were reviewing text-books that he had not read, his daily lessons were often of double length.

"Nothing hurts me more than to flunk or

fizzle, and again, nothing does me more good, for on the next lesson, I always study till I know it, even though I see the next day, before I go to bed.　Dr. Taylor is very considerate, and will excuse me on all that I have not before read ; but I hate to ask him, or to be excused at all.　I never was in a better school.　And I will not give up, if I study every night till morning.

"Last night, at seven, I commenced to study on the lesson for New Year's day ; with the exception of fifteen minutes, I studied hard until a quarter of one (1861).　I never saw the old year out so before ; but I saw every word of that Greek out, and then went to bed.

"I have not been able to retire before eleven, any night this week ; twice I have been up till nearly one, and twice I got up at half after four.　I intend to take a good stand as a scholar, unless I make myself sick in the attempt.

"Father writes to me to be sure and take eight hours sleep, every day, and plenty of exercise. This is what we call, 'morally impossible,' in view of two pages daily of Greek, or one hundred and forty lines of Virgil, to be recited to Dr. Taylor."

It was a natural sequence of all this, that his old enemy, the headache, which was put to the rout at the agricultural school, should return with violence; and great was the relief when he could relax these efforts, and report, " there is now no doubt of my ability to hold my place in the senior class."

With this force of will and this zeal in study, was united strength of moral purpose in regard to the ordinary temptations of student-life. In reply to my request for some positive assurance that he would avoid that special bane of the student,—scenes of conviviality, in which the cigar and the wine-cup tempt to idleness, wastefulness, and excess,—he writes :

" I can say, honestly, that I NEVER ' took a drink' of any intoxicating or other liquor. And I willingly promise that I never will ; for I detest it from the bottom of my heart.

"As to tobacco, I have used it, as you know. I can say nothing in its defence, except as a pleasure; and those who have never smoked cannot appreciate that. It seems but a little thing for you to ask me to give it up; and it is, compared with what I ask of you; but it is *terribly hard*.

"I will promise not to use it, in any form, while at Andover, and if ever again, I will let you see me the first time. I trust I shall be able to keep this promise. The academy pledge I should probably have broken; but I will be true to you."

XI.

MARCH 4, 1861. " To-day Lincoln begins his important career. I hope he will do his best to punish some of the traitors now in office."

April 22. " There is great excitement here [Andover] about the times. A company is now forming in town, and the military spirit runs high. Dr. Taylor does not consider it our duty to enlist at present, and he advises us to do nothing rashly. But he approves the forming of a company in school, of such as are capable of bearing arms, for practice and the learning of military tactics. In virtue of my graduation at Russell's, I shall probably have an office, perhaps a high one, and will you do me the favor to send by mail an edition of Scott's Manual for infantry? I feel quite excited, and want to enlist."

To this I replied that the exigency did not yet require that students should abandon their whole life-plan for the present defence of the country ; that, from the nature of the conflict and of the territory upon which it must be waged, the desperation of the rebel leaders, and the persistent malignity of the slave-power, the war must last for at least three years ; that just now the rush of volunteers was greater than the President had called for ; but that the war would be no holiday affair, and the time might come when I must bid him go, and when he must be ready to take every risk ; adding, " I hope you will become perfect in drill, so that if called to go, you may be fully prepared."

He was elected captain of the "Ellsworth" or Phillips Cadets—a company of some seventy academy boys, whose daily drills gave a new life to Andover Hill during the summer of 1861. The *Andover Advertiser* makes frequent mention of " Capt. Thompson's" proficiency. Under this responsibility, he writes :

" I thank you for the Manuals. I am studying them continually, and practicing with my company. We have two drills a week from Captain Oliver, U. S. A., and ours is the best drilled company in town. I am trying to go farther than mere head-work, by a private drill daily with a heavy musket I have borrowed. It is fine exercise, and good for my own military training, as I am careful to learn every motion rightly and on time. I am strong for war ; it seems to me that the South needs a lesson which cannot be taught by 'compromise' or 'starvation.'

" Do you want me to go, or do you only not object if it be necessary ? I stand ready to go at once, if I can find a suitable place. Should a dozen of our boys volunteer, I would be one ; but it would be hard to enlist in a strange company that one knows

nothing about. I think, when there is another call, and colleges and schools respond,
Phillips boys will not be behind.

"We all find it very hard to study, and
Dr. Taylor doesn't get cross."

His own judicious management of the
company did much to secure the favorable
consideration of the Principal for what
might easily have become a serious cause of
distraction in the school.

"He was always so true and manly in his
deportment," writes Dr. S. H. Taylor,* "so
considerate in whatever he supposed might
involve any irregularity in the school, that
he secured my warm interest and entire confidence. In the company connected with the
academy, there were from time to time
plans and projects started that might be
supposed to interfere with the general plan
or course of study in the school, but he was
so thoughtful in regard to all these, that as
commander, he would never have one of them
put to vote till he had consulted me; and

* Principal of Phillips Academy, Andover, Mass.

then, if my views were different from his wishes, with a generous and manly spirit, without the least appearance of opposition he complied with what I thought best. So in regard to everything else connected with the school, he was all that I could have desired. I can now recall nothing in his whole deportment which I could have wished otherwise. You can well imagine, then, that even in the midst of the hurry and cares of the closing days of the term, the news of his death was most painful to me.

"The remembrance of your son will always be sweet. He died in the service of the country, and he died a Christian—two circumstances which involve more true nobleness than all things else."

A dear friend,* who often watched from his garden the boy-captain drilling his company upon the opposite green, and who had also a personal knowledge of his character, writes:

"Your noble boy we all knew well enough

---

* Professor Austin Phelps, D. D.

to love him and trust him. His quiet manliness won our hearts, and we have often spoken of him in our family circle as one of the few young friends whose military career we watched anxiously and hopefully."

And another honored divine of New England, among the foremost of her patriots,* sends this reminiscence of the academy captain :

"Two years since, when attending the examination of the theological students at Andover, I there saw your son at the head of a company of the young men in the academy. After drilling them for some time, he marched them to the front of the Mansion House, where they were paraded in honor of some of the trustees who were at that time present. His manly air, his skilful drilling, and his graceful military salute to the trustees, as the governors of the institution, are still fresh before me. A few days since, my eye glanced casually at a newspaper announcement of his decease, and I can

Rev. W. T. Dwight, D. D., Portland, Maine.

now easily recognize in the young soldier of the 106th N. Y. S. V., who has so early fought the good fight of Christian patriotism, the more youthful leader of Andover Hill.

" The loss of such a son must awaken the bitterness of a father's grief. While you have reason to bless God that you have had such a son to give up to our suffering country, you need, and I doubt not you have received, strength sufficient to prevent you from falling utterly for the time.

" To fight this monstrous treason and perjury is as sacred a duty as to send missionaries to the heathen; and it seems to demand more submission, more simple trust, when the young soldier falls prematurely, than when the missionary is thus removed. But, in the view of God, your dear son is as truly a conqueror as if the last battle had been fought and the last army of the rebellion cut down. He has gone up soon to receive his reward, far sooner than you looked for, but to as blessed a rest as if a veteran from a hundred conflicts.

"Patient, serene courage; disinterested consecration to one's country, because God is thus served; and a filial trust the groundwork of all—no exhibition of youthful worth can be more attractive or powerful in its influence. Your son, being dead, still speaks, and with more energy than if he were still on earth.

"Not a few young soldiers of the cross who entered our armies with a similar spirit have, like him, already exchanged the sword of earthly conflict for the palm of the conqueror above. Our country knows not how to part with them, but Heaven is the happier for every such addition to her chosen ones."

XII.

THE warrior shades of ancient Greece must have been stirred with a bewildering jargon of time and place, as the Phillips seniors of 1861, on graduation day, were enrolled as a company of Greek Skirmishers, and drilled by Hardee's Tactics done into Greek by "*Abrocomas*, the Chief General." The audience, however, seemed conscious of no anachronism in this sudden transformation of the captain of the Ellsworth Cadets, who put his spearmen and bowmen in battle array against the Megarians as promptly as if they had been but going through an everyday drill in front of the Seminary.

It was not strange that a youth who had spent two years at a military school, and

7*   (77)

had elicited the commendation of military
men for his skillful handling of a company,
should feel himself called to serve his country in arms, and more competent to serve
her in this capacity than some newly-com-
missioned officers. Said Dr. Taylor, who
had a fatherly interest in his success at College, "If John makes up his mind that it
is his *duty* to enter the army, nothing can
hold him back."

And, surely, no Christian patriot would
seek, upon any personal grounds, to hold
back a son qualified to bear arms, from the
defense of the nation in this great conflict
for Constitutional liberty, for human freedom, and for Christian civilization. But
in his case, at that time, there were many
things to be considered in determining the
question of duty. Not yet nineteen years
of age, of a slender constitution, impaired
anew by the severe application of the winter, it was doubtful whether he could really
be of service in the camp or the field. It
seemed possible, also, that his eagerness to

enlist was but a boyish enthusiasm, caught by sympathy, which might fail under the test of hardship. Moreover, it is indispensable to the welfare of the country that, even in times of war, a portion of her sons should be in training for future service in the educated professions; and while in a certain sense man counts for man in such a struggle, yet to detach these from an unfinished course of education, and set them upon the work of present defense, would be a more serious detriment to the permanent interests of the nation, than the withdrawal of an equal number of farmers or artisans from manual labor.

This was clearly seen by that foremost patriot of the American Revolution, John Adams, when he counseled Mr. Jonathan Mason, who had been entered as a student in his law office, to continue at his books, notwithstanding the commotions of the opening Revolution. No sooner had the news of the Declaration of Independence reached Boston, than young Mason, fired with martial enthusiasm, wrote to Mr. Adams, proposing to relinquish his studies and to take up arms for the country. Writing from Philadelphia, the very center of Revolutionary fervor, on the 18th July, 1776, Mr. Adams says :

" I cannot advise you to quit the retired scene of which you have hitherto appeared to be so fond, and engage in the noisy business of war. I doubt not you have honor and spirit and abilities sufficient to make a figure in the field ; and if the future circumstances of your country should make it necessary, I hope you would not hesitate to buckle on your armor. But at present I see no necessity for it. Accomplishments of the civil and political kind are no less necessary for the happiness of mankind than martial ones. We cannot all be soldiers ; and there will probably be, in a very few years, a greater scarcity of lawyers and statesmen than of warriors.

" The circumstances of this country from the years 1755 to 1758, during which period

I was a student in Mr. Putnam's office, were almost as confused as they are now, and the prospect before me, my young friend, was much more gloomy than yours. I felt an inclination exactly similar to yours, for engaging in active martial life, but I was advised, and, upon a consideration of all circumstances, concluded, to mind my books. Whether my determination was prudent or not, it is not possible to say, but I never repented it."

Clearly then, as matters stood during the first six months of the present war, there was no urgency for the enlistment of minors engaged in a special course of education.

But this young aspirant for military service felt his inward call. To prove his power of endurance, he made the tour of the White Mountains on foot, walking fifteen and twenty miles a day, with a knapsack on his shoulders and a gun in his hand. His capacity for useful service, as shown by his success in the Andover organization, he urged as his chief reason for wishing to en-

ter the army.   And as for study, he had no
thought of relinquishing a college education,
but would return to that after the war.
There seemed also a Providential opening
in the offer of a New England Governor
who had witnessed his Andover drills, to
give him a commission in a regiment just
starting for the South.

Yet with all this strength of desire and
of conviction, such was his deference toward
his natural advisers, that when I said to
him, "My opinion is that in the present
surplusage of volunteers,* students are not
called upon to give up college for the army,
—but here is the money for your outfit at
either; go to Concord and get your commission, or go to New Haven and enter
Yale;"—he went alone to think, and I
doubt not to pray, and, on returning, said,
" Father, I *do wish* to enter the army, and I
feel that there is the place for me ; but as
you seem to prefer it, I will go to college."

Believing that another year's development

* September, 1861.

of brain and muscle would make him so much the better soldier, if that should prove to be his calling, I was content to leave the final settlement of the question to whatever opportunity or emergency might afterwards arise ; and so he entered college in good faith, though with abated zeal.

He does not study "very hard," nor aim to take more than a "fair" stand—for his heart is enlisted in another service. Still he "has study enough to keep him busy," and in the general, college-life moves on pleasantly and prosperously. . . . "I like Herodotus quite well ; I think I do like Greek pretty well, *considering.* I try to make the best of everything, but most earnestly wish that 'peculiar circumstances' would let me enter the army. I would start to-night if I could."

Seeking the best wisdom for him and for myself, I commended him to the thoughtful and patriotic counsels of my most tried and faithful friend, Rev. Leonard Bacon, D.D. of New Haven.

"I have had a talk with John," wrote
Dr. B. in reply, "but found that I was not
likely to make much impression by the ar-
guments which I used to dissuade him from
interrupting the course of his education.
My object in talking with him was not so
much to influence him as to know the state
of his mind.

"I do not see how you can wisely over-
rule or obviate his strong inclination. What
the Providence of God intends concerning
him, we cannot foresee. But if he were my
son, and I could not change his mind—if I
saw that the impulse was strong upon him,
and was making study and all peaceful pursuits distasteful to him,—I think I should
be compelled to say, however reluctantly,
'It is of the Lord.' Perhaps God has purposes concerning him which our short-sight-
ed wisdom would baffle if it could. We
must say in such cases, 'The will of the
Lord be done.'

"Perhaps it would be well for you to put
him upon an examination of his own motives

—whether he wants to undertake this military service from mere restlessness, from the spirit of adventure, or from higher motives and in the spirit of self-sacrifice.

"I will only add that I was much pleased with the modest manliness of his bearing in the whole conversation. Should he go into the army, I think he will be found every inch a man. When my sons went, my feeling was, Somebody's sons must go, and why not mine? May God direct you and bless you in this dear son and in all your children!"

As the result of this interview, John—who, in common with his father, was seeking to know the will of God in this matter—determined to rest his final decision upon an application to Governor Buckingham for a commission as lieutenant. This conclusion he communicates in these playful words:

"To-morrow evening I will send to the Governor of this State a series of documents from yourself, Uncle D., Mr. Russell, Dr.

8

Bacon, etc., etc., showing all my good qualities ; (each letter of the above named to be,
in fact, an *essay* on some particular good
quality, so as to have no waste of recom-
mendation by repetition!) These the Governor will read, and, if he gives me an appointment, well and good ; if not, I will drop
the subject and devote myself to Latin, and
worse Greek, and worse still algebra ; that
is, if I pass the examination next week.
This soup remains to be served. This is my
final decision, to which,

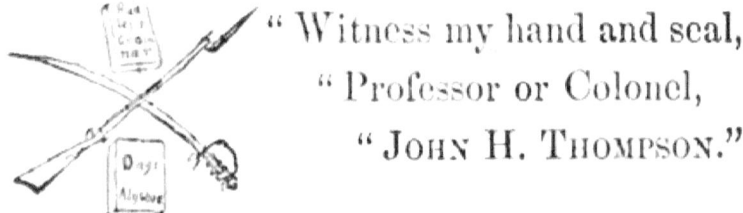

      " Witness my hand and seal,

        " Professor or Colonel,

          " JOHN H. THOMPSON."

    When the Governor replied that he had
no vacancy, the predestined soldier wrote,
" Because the Governor did not send me
a commission as brigadier-general, or even
first-lieutenant, I see no reason to infer that
the will of Providence is against me." But
that will was not yet made plain.

    The interest of Governor Buckingham in

his application is most kindly expressed in the following note of April 9, 1863 :

"DEAR SIR :—My thanks for your favor of the 26th inst., respecting the death of your noble son.

"I remember him with perfect distinctness, and regretted at the time he called on me I saw no way in which I could commission him in a Connecticut regiment, and secure to the honor of the State the services of so pure a Christian patriot. Allow me to express my deep sympathy with you and your family in the irreparable loss you have sustained.

"This is one of the strong proofs of the criminality of this rebellion—one of the sacrifices necessary for its suppression. What a cost to our nation! But the compensation will, I doubt not, be the deliverance of the captive, the extension of the principles of civil liberty, and the more complete and perfect security for personal rights.

"Allow me to rejoice with you in the rich

consolation which you have respecting the
consecration of your noble son not only to
the interests of his country, but to the cause
of Christ.

    " With much sympathy,

        " Believe me very truly yours,

           " WM. A. BUCKINGHAM."

XIII.

ON the 25th day of May, 1862, General
Banks, whose forces had been seriously
reduced by the demands of General Mc
Clellan's campaign on the peninsula, was
driven down the Shenandoah valley by
the superior numbers of Stonewall Jackson's army, and the alarm was sounded from
Washington that the capital was in danger.
Several regiments of State militia at once
volunteered for three months' service—
among these the 22d regiment of New York
National Guards. The exigency upon which
the long-coveted enlistment was made to
hinge had plainly arisen, and the boy's heart
was wild with joy when a telegram, signed
with his father's name, summoned him to lay

down his books and to take up his musket. His classmates had never seen him so jubilant even in the merriest of college sports. In twenty-four hours he was enrolled as a private in Company G. of the 22d, and was on his way to join the regiment at Baltimore. It was well for father and son that both had so long and carefully weighed the question of duty, that when this new peril of the country came there was nothing left but for the one to say Go, and for the other to march.

Though not much given to personal intimacies, yet in his nine months' stay at Yale, John had favorably impressed his classmates by the same qualities that had marked his early school life. The fellow-student who stood nearest in his confidence thus sums up that brief college career:

"Your son was highly respected by the class, and esteemed by all who became acquainted with him. Among his classmates he was very reserved, never obtrusive, and admired by all for his manly bearing and gentlemanly deportment. Among the members of his own Division he was a great favorite, and won praise from all by his mirth and pleasant manner. He was, as we are accustomed to say, the life of his Division, and I think, if he could have remained with us during the course, he would have become very popular ; and I know, as our acquaintance ripened into intimacy, that he would have been respected by the class, and the recipient of its honors.

"In the studies of the college he never professed any brilliant attainments, nor did he attempt any display. He preferred other things ; and, in fact, from the very commencement of his college course, he seemed, in one sense, a stranger to us, and doubtless duty called him elsewhere. He never entered with zeal into study, because his heart and soul were, as I understood him, enlisted in another and nobler cause, in the service of which he hoped to enroll his name. He always seemed restless and impatient under the restraint, longing for the word to go to

battle ; and when I think how delighted he
was in entering the service in the humblest
capacity, I cannot believe otherwise than
that his motives sprung from the purest and
most patriotic sources ; and were I able to
relate the many conversations we have had
on the subject, his own words would be the
strongest proof of his sincerity. We, who
knew him and were under him at Andover,
can testify that he merited other situations.
He was the first representative of his class
in the war, and we take pleasure that he
was such."

The class itself expressed its appreciation
of him in the following tribute :

" WHEREAS, we have heard with heartfelt
sorrow of the death of our late classmate,
JOHN HANSON THOMPSON, while in the service of his country ; therefore,

" *Resolved*, That we, his classmates, have
lost in his death a warm friend and genial
companion ; and our country, a devoted patriot.

" *Resolved*, That we, who knew him well,

can testify to the earnest patriotism and
noble ambition which impelled him to leave
books and friends that he might devote his
life and labor to his country.

" *Resolved*, That we tender to his bereaved
family our sincere sympathy and condolence.

" *Resolved*, That the class wear the usual
badge of mourning for thirty days ; and
that a committee of six be appointed to attend the funeral ; also, that a copy of these
resolutions be sent to his family, and to the
daily papers of New Haven, and to the Yale
Literary Magazine, for publication.

XIV.

HIS first experience of camp life might have dampened his ardor, but for the thoroughness of his conviction that duty called him to serve his country in any capacity : and so, after a night spent in rain and mud, and a heavy morning's task in digging trenches, carrying the loads of soil upon a board, for lack of a wheelbarrow, he says, cheerily, "Now all this is extremely 'rough ;' but it is jolly, if one takes it right." After a few days, the regiment was ordered to Harper's Ferry, then a post of danger. "I am very glad, indeed," he writes. "We may be brought into active service—may not. I will not speculate where I know nothing. But, whatever may come, I am

(94)

ready—it is what I came for. I have been happy thus far, and shall not complain at any orders. We take one day's rations, and each man twenty rounds of ball cartridge ; so we are ready for anything, and hurrying on. Much love to all ; and, as I know not what may come, Good-bye to one and all."

The three months' enlistment passed quietly in Camp Aspinwall, at Bolivar, with just enough of rumors and alarms to keep the Twenty-second on the *qui vive*, without testing its pluck in an engagement. The routine of guard and picket duty, the daily drill, with occasional special exercises in connection with a company of artillery posted near the camp, gave our young private a thorough "breaking in" for a soldier's life ; while the harder service of the pick and the spade, to which he was subjected in digging entrenchments, and the open-air exposure to heat and cold, rain, wind and mud, tested both his physical endurance and his martial enthusiasm.

With scrupulous attention to personal cleanliness, frequent bathing, the avoidance of noxious habits, and a "merry heart," cheerful in the consciousness of duty, calm in its reliance upon God, he maintained a tone of health and of spirits that threw over his daily letters the charm of the surrounding rivers, woods and mountains, in their sunniest hours.

"I am enjoying myself, and growing strong and brown. One gets accustomed to sleeping and waking 'to order;' and, when one can lie down on a bare board, and in two minutes be soundly and comfortably asleep, he must be either tired or not particular."

"August 7th. Father's birth-day! Turn out the guard! Present arms! Allow me to congratulate you on the happy termination of your — year.

"One son having passed through a complete course of youthful instruction—a tour in Europe, all boarding and public schools, the Yale Scientific, and, lastly, an elaborate course in Yale itself—now takes his stand in the noble cause of his country, and toils in the trenches in the mud of the 'sacred soil.'"

But, with all his *bonhomie*, of which this is a characteristic specimen, he does not forget to write of the prayer meetings, nightly at his captain's tent—"interesting and *sensible* meetings," and inspiriting by the numbers in attendance, and by the music of the soldiers' hymns.

He writes to a sister, "Do not fear that I smoke too much, or that I shall fall into bad habits. I have promised not to play cards—or I did promise before I went to college—and I have kept my word thus far."

The moral tone of the regiment, and the personal character of his tent-mates, favored his desire to maintain an upright and consistent Christian walk amid the dissipating influences of camp life. Indeed, the reputation of the Twenty-second for gentlemanly virtues seems indelibly impressed upon the residents of Harper's Ferry. The owner of a small fruit garden near Bolivar said to me, recently, "That Twenty-second was the best regiment ever sent here. *They didn't steal!*" Certainly, private Thompson of Company G, always counted himself fortunate in his association with such "jolly, good fellows," who, while relishing fun and working manfully, maintained in the tent and the camp, the courtesies of the gentleman and the graces of the Christian. What Company G thought of their young recruit their own resolutions testify ; in which they "deeply deplore the early death of one who gave promise of so much usefulness, and who, by the transparent sincerity and truthfulness of his character, by his unvarying courtesy and kindness of disposition, by his unassuming modesty, and by the manifestation of all the traits that mark the true Christian gentleman, had become greatly endeared to all of us, who rejoice to remember him as comrade and friend—as a soldier, prompt, ready, active and obedient ; as a friend, true, earnest and sincere."

The Company voted to inscribe his name on the roll of its Honorary Members, with the words—

"𝕯𝖎𝖊𝖉 𝖎𝖓 𝖙𝖍𝖊 𝕾𝖊𝖗𝖛𝖎𝖈𝖊 𝖔𝖋 𝕳𝖎𝖘 𝕮𝖔𝖚𝖓𝖙𝖗𝖞."

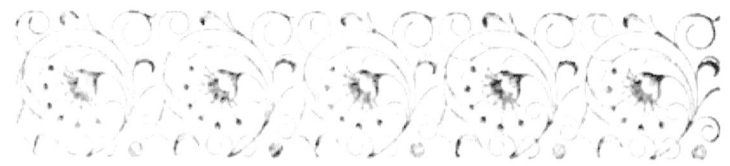

XV.

AUGUST 23, 1862.—"In looking back over the last three months, I can only feel glad that I have had the experience here, and do not grudge the sacrifices made. I am in better health and spirits than when I started. And in looking forward, I have for a few days considered the whole subject carefully, and think I had better go again, for three years or the war,—that it is my duty to go.

"This is the sum of all. I have always wanted to go to the war. After long waiting, I have tried the experiment. And having seen the hardest service, except a fight, I leave it to you whether my letters have been grumbling complaints.

"I am in for it, and like it; but as to re-enlisting, if you 'don't see it,' I will do my duty in college, as heretofore."

One so ready to do his duty, in any sphere, could not be long in learning to what sphere he was now called. Of course, he did not wish to re-enlist as a private, though willing to do even that, if his country's need required it; but he felt himself competent for a higher post. "I may say, without boasting, that I have a better theoretical knowledge of, and have had more practice in, all military movements, than half of our officers; while, for general education, my advantages have been far better, whatever my knowledge may be. I have tried thoroughly to understand all military tactics.

"I can not think it is my duty to go as a private for three years, as long as we have so many ignorant officers. As an officer, it would be my duty to go, because I think I know enough, and have the full spirit of the thing, and don't care much for anything else."

9*

His aspirations, however, were not high, and were based more upon the conviction of a capacity to serve, than upon a desire of personal distinction. A sergeantcy would suit well enough, and this post was offered him him in the One Hundred and Eleventh New York State Volunteers, just as the term of the Twenty-second National Guard expired. It was necessary, however, that he should return to New York, and be mustered out, before enlisting anew, and this led to a series of adventures that proved his patience, courage and enthusiasm in his vocation.

On the very day when he should have reached his new regiment at Harper's Ferry, Lee's army invaded Maryland at the Monocacy, and the train in which the sergeant left Baltimore was stopped at that point by the destruction of the bridge. As the train approached the scene of danger, he loaded his revolver and went forward to the locomotive, to keep an eye upon the engineer, concerning whose loyalty a suspicion had been started among the passengers. By the

time the cars returned to Baltimore, that
excitable city had been placed under martial
law, and hardly had the sergeant left the
depot, when he was arrested by a mounted
patrol of the provost-guard, and with a lot
of ragamuffins, scoured up from the streets,
was marched ignominiously to the guard-
house, some two or three miles distant.
Being in soldier's dress, but without arms,
and having no descriptive papers,—for Red
Tape had no printed form of mustering out
on hand, at the New York head-quarters, and
he had expected to be mustered in at Harper's
Ferry,—he was presumed to be a deserter,
and had nothing but his honest face to cer-
tify his statement.

As he humorously describes it : "While I
stood in front of the depot,

> Lo! from afar there came a band,
> With one that midst them stately rode,
> A leader in the land ;—

who reined up his steed, and shouted, ' Halloa
you! have you a pass?' 'No, sir.' 'Fall

in, then.' The bugle sounded forward ; **and**
at once your son was receiving the honors
of Baltimore, marching through the crowded
streets with a body-guard of twenty-five
mounted men, with drawn sabres, **ten upon**
each side, and the others closing up front
and rear ;—a horse-thief just before **him,**
drunken stragglers around him, and he himself having 'nary document' nor friend to
back him."

After long waiting, with the prospect of
a night in dismal and dirty quarters, he succeeded in getting a hearing, which resulted
in his being marched from office to office,
until he was given into the custody of the
guard to be conveyed to fort McHenry!
Up to this point he had borne the affair
with good-humored patience, forbearing to
aggravate his blundering captors by protes-
tations or complaints ; but **now** he demanded
to be conducted to the commander of the
post for a personal investigation. At this
the marshal ordered him back to the hotel
where his knapsack was deposited, there to

remain under guard. Fortunately, he met a friend who gained access to General Wool, and procured for him a pass to return to New York.

By this time Red Tape had succeeded in obtaining from Washington a printed form of discharge from service in the 22d; and fortified with this and with a pass, the sergeant set out immediately by way of Harrisburgh for Wheeling, hoping in this way to reach the 111th and assume his post in season for the impending battle. But at Cumberland he found that he could proceed no further—the communication being intercepted upon that side also;—and thus he was spared the feeling of a personal disgrace in the surrender of Harper's Ferry. All this time he was giving his whole energy, at his own expense, to the attempt to serve his country in the field, while states, cities and towns were lavishing bounty-money to attract recruits. In his letters of this date he pleasantly signs himself the "Would-be-sergeant seeking for a chance to fight."

At Cumberland he volunteered his services in drilling the citizens, and in other measures of defence against a rumored rebel invasion. He did good, also, as he had opportunity—affectionately warning a young officer whom he saw under the effects of liquor, of the danger and the shame of such indulgence; and giving words of sympathy and comfort to the sick and wounded in hospital. Having taken up the vocation of a soldier as a religious duty, he never lost sight of its grave responsibilities; and the enthusiasm and vivacity with which he entered upon his work was tempered by the thoughtful forecasting of possibilities. In describing the general hospital at Clear Spring, near Cumberland—its healthy location and the excellent management of the surgeons,—he adds, "I looked with interest on this hospital-work, for my service in these parts may sometime end there, for a time at least."

While waiting at Cumberland for the coveted opportunity of service, he attracted

the notice of a captain in the 106th N. Y.
S. V., then stationed at New Creek, who
offered him a sergeantcy in Company A of
that regiment, where his true military life
began, and in which he continued till its
close.

XVI.

"I HAD seen a notice of the death of your son in the *Evening Post*," writes an honored friend who himself has rendered to the country the highest personal services and sacrifices,—"and Mrs. L. had cut it out to be sent with other slips to my son in Louisiana, but little did we think that the name Thompson, there, was your own family name. The '*Sergeant* Thompson' made a deep impression upon us. It sounded so manly and so patriotic when every one who has some education strives for a commission."*

It was his own conviction that his knowledge of the manual could be used to the best

* Professor Francis Lieber, LL.D.

advantage in the position of a non-commissioned drill-officer, and he determined to begin with doing faithfully the particular work that he understood.

On the 20th Sept. 1862, he writes from New Creek Station, Va., " I am happy to state that I am just about in the position where I have tried to place myself for the last two weeks. After all my various luck, ill and good, I have found a home for three years: Capt. P. offers me a second sergeantcy in his company. This is not as high as was offered at Harper's Ferry, but I don't want to fight Indians in the West with paroled prisoners. 1, 2, 3, How about that 111th? So I shall accept this offer, and if I am 2nd sergeant for the war, it is only my fault. If I rise to a commission it is my own glory."

His competence and energy soon won for him the confidence of both officers and men. The regiment was one of new recruits, and the absence of some of its officers devolved upon others much extra service, especially in the heavy picket duty that the post required. For a time the newly-enlisted sergeant had almost the entire instruction of his company, then stationed on the Knobly mountain, two miles from camp. As fidelity in small things, and the habit of prompt and implicit obedience are prime qualities in a soldier, his method of training furnishes a good illustration of both.

"I am doing the best I can to teach the men all things in the most exact manner. I drill them five hours daily.

"It is hard work to manage some of the men; that is, they are old and want *reasons* for everything. If I say 'you must remove the paper from the cartridge before loading,' some one says, 'I never load that way, I shan't do it.' '*Sir!* put that ball in without the paper.' 'Why?' 'Because I tell you to;'—and at last, in goes the ball.

"'Company, fall in for drill!' 'Where are we going?' 'Never mind where you are going, *fall in,*' say I. And though I often have to repeat orders, and repeat again, I never had a man refuse to obey, and always after he has obeyed I tell him all I can to explain his trouble. But they are learning rapidly to obey promptly. At night I always post the Camp Guard. I have the countersign and go round to each sentry and give him full instructions, and often if I wake up at two or three o'clock, I go round and see how things are.

"The Captain, or 1st Lieutenant acting captain in command, puts a great deal of confidence in me ; he never drills the men nor attends to Guard mounting. All I do is to try and do my duty to the fullest extent, in hope that all will go well."

With him the daily drill was never a matter of mere regulation routine, but, appreciating its importance, he sought in this, as in every thing he undertook, the highest attainable excellence. "I saw the dress-parade of the Twenty-third Illinois, Col. Mulligan's Irish Brigade, and they equal the Seventh New York. It roused me a good deal, and so I put Company A through

the next time ; for two hours I kept them in
a regular hard drill. It is quite amusing
to hear the men talk : 'Sergeant, if you drill
us much longer, we shall beat the regiment,'
etc. ; 'Sergeant. I never was drilled before
I saw you.' The other companies are under
drill-masters, lieutenants, etc., from Mulligan's Brigade, so it is quite a race for me to
see whether Company A, in spite of all its
hard guard duties, can not beat the other
companies when again we meet."

This laudable ambition soon had its reward. " Yesterday was Company A's first
appearance on dress-parade, and I have the
satisfaction of learning from many sources
that, in all respects, 'we' were equal to the
other companies, and that in our 'order
arms' we surpassed the whole. I do not
tell this to boast, but because it is a great
gratification to me to know that, if I am
now sick, Company A first got some good
from me.

" Do not, by any means, imagine that, in
three weeks or three years, I am to be made

second lieutenant in this company. All the other sergeants have prior claims, for their aid in recruiting and because they are from the regiment's native county. I only desire to do my full duty, whether as sergeant, drill-master, or whatever position I may occupy. I have not asked for promotion, nor talked of it, either to my officers or fellow sergeants."

The benefits of this persevering drill-work soon appeared in his ready handling of the company upon a night-alarm, in the absence of the captain and other officers. "Night before last we had an alarm in camp. I went to the sentry with Sergeant C., and found that he had fired at a man who was skulking round and refused to answer the challenge. C. and I started down the hill and searched the bushes, but found no one. I went back and reported. Lieut. D. turned out the guard, and left the company in my care. I formed company, loaded, fixed bayonets, and then made them 'mark time,' to keep warm, and to cool them

10*

off. By the time D. returned, I had a cool and ready company. He took half, and left me in charge of the rest and of the camp, the men to lie in ranks just under the hill. After scouting for some two hours, we returned to our bunks. I presume that some bushwackers were 'feeling us,' to see how quickly we could turn out."

A strong mark of the confidence of his superior officers in his courage, fidelity, and discretion, was given in the incident which is here described in his own words:—

"One misty, rainy morning, as I was sitting in my tent, just after breakfast, the flap was unceremoniously thrown open, and Major P., our captain, called out, 'Halloa, Sergeant! Why haven't you reported at the colonel's headquarters?'

"'Because I was not ordered to do so.' I was expecting some joke from the major, as is his habit.

"'Well, go up and report at once; you are to go to Cumberland.'

"I went up, and the colonel said, 'Ser-

geant, you are to go to Cumberland with
the rebel captain. Have you a good revolver?"

"'Yes, sir.'

"'Go to your quarters and get ready;
then report here.'

"I went to the carall and got two
horses, and then to the provost headquarters
and found the captain. He was a fine looking fellow, about thirty, strong, well built,
and very pleasant.

"'Captain, I am to take you to Cumberland; your horse is waiting now.'

"'Is any one going beside yourself?'

"'No, sir; I am detailed to take you to
Cumberland. Here is my order: 'Sergeant
Thompson will proceed to Cumberland on
horseback, and deliver to General Kelly the
person of Moses O'Brien, a deserter from
the rebel service,' etc. Captain, if you go
with me quietly, and make no attempt to
escape, I will do well by you; but, if I see
the least motion, a quickening of the pace
of your horse, or any thing that looks like

an attempt to escape, I shall shoot you at once. You see, here is my loaded Colt's; you are unarmed, and it will be strange if I can't put *one* of the six balls through you before you get off.'

"'Very well, sir. I shall go quietly, for I have no desire to escape.'

"As my prisoner was buckling on his spurs, I suggested that I would like to wear one myself, whereupon he at once unbuckled and I put the spur on. We then mounted, and were off.

"'Hope you will come back safely, Sergeant,' cried some one.

"'I will.'

"I had no more idea of the road than you have; but I knew it could not diverge much from the railroad. The distance was about twenty-four miles or less; the road, the first half, was awful—mud, rocks, rivers to ford. the Potomac, the water nearly to my feet. We came soon to a gate, and I suggested that the captain might dismount and open it, as my orders were strict.

"For a time we rode in silence, and then, as the captain seemed pleasant, I entered into conversation, and he gave me much information in regard to rebeldom and his own adventures.

"He had been with Ashby, but lately belonged to the Seventeenth Battalion cavalry. He deserted from Harper's Ferry, by means of a sick-furlough. I had very interesting conversation all along, keeping my eye on him. At about noon we came to Rawlings, and as we approached a neat farm-house, I proposed dining. The captain said he had no money, but I told him that it was by my invitation. We had quite a fine farm-dinner for twenty-five cents each. I said nothing of our relative position, and they did not suspect my secesh, though the grey-back and gilt braid was before them.

"We then mounted and rode on through a much better country and a better road, along the hillside. We passed some fine farms on the plains, mostly cultivated though not very thoroughly, as farming seems to be at a discount here. As soon as harvest is over, the men go hunting and let the farms rot till spring, hence, there is no advance or improvement. Of course there are exceptions, and I saw a few good farms and houses. At last we neared the railroad, and a mountain seemed to close up all outlets, but the road went one side and the railroad the other. Here we found a picket, the outpost from Cumberland, and over the hill, or rather from the top of the hill we saw Cumberland, about a mile off.

"I lent the captain my rubber coat in order to hide the heavy gilt braid on his grey-back coat. So pulling on his new acquisition, he rode into the town without drawing a crowd. We went at once to Kelly's headquarters, I knowing full well where they were, and tying our animals, I marched my charge up stairs and presented him. It seems that we came at just the time for good luck to the captain, if his assertions were true, for after a half hour's talk and a few questions as to his whence and whither and wherefore, the General allowed him to take the oath of allegiance and go in peace. We took rooms together at the St. Nicholas, and then a good supper; after which, the sergeant swelled round the hotel, talking with his old friends. He thought of former days when he was only a private in that hotel, but now an exalted sergeant, ahem!

"The next morning after breakfast, I attended to some few errands, paid my bill, received my orders and pass from the General, said good-bye to my captain, got my horse and was off at ten o'clock. I strapped my coat to the saddle and put my spur to the horse, and made some good time on the level ground.

"I reached camp in safety at about five o'clock; gave the return order to Colonel James, put up my 'animal,' returning once more to the bosom of my family and the embraces of our mess. The captain's *spur* now mine, shall be duly preserved and adorn my future home. My future wife, whoever she may be, shall have the pleasure of dusting it and thinking on the perils of a twenty-three-mile ride with a stout rebel deserter."

From the manner in which he fulfilled this trust. I was not surprised to hear a captain in his regiment say. " the eye of his commanding officer was upon him, and he was designated for promotion to the first vacancy." But it was grateful to hear from the lips of his colonel, as we stood together beside his silent form. " Your son was a complete soldier, and a model gentleman. I had already made out his commission as lieutenant."

Indeed his young reputation had extended beyond his own camp. A friend writes : " My brother, Gen. J. J. Bartlett, had upon inquiry become so favorably acquainted with your son's character and standing in the army, that he had determined to offer him a position on his staff, in case of a vacancy expected." And he adds, " you have such a precious bequest in the Christian character and public services of a child, it almost touches the condolence with thanks-giving, that in obedience to God's and our country's call for a contribution, you had so much to give."*

* Rev. W. A. Bartlett, of Brooklyn.

11

XVII.

THE tactical drill, while of the first consequence in the mind of an officer, by no means completes the round of his daily duties in the camp. The health and comfort, the amusement and instruction of the men, will engage much of his attention. And it is in the every-day life of the soldier, rather than upon the battle-field, that one sees the best examples of patient courage and of personal fidelity. The good soldier learns to make light of his privations, and even to extract pleasure from them; and the faithful officer will bring all the resources of his mind and the advantages of his education to bear upon the physical, social and moral improvement of his men.

At first the non-commissioned officers of Company A tented together, thus securing for themselves some extra comforts, and enjoying much pleasurable intercourse. "Five such abolition, slavery-hating, vigorous-prosecution-of-the-war fellows you never saw in any one space, ten by ten." Their evenings were given to studies and discussions in science, literature and economics;—geology and history being pursued in the way of regular recitations.

"We have just closed our debate, a very interesting and I think profitable one ; the common question of George Washington and Columbus—which deserves the most praise. It rubs up our patriotism and acts as a general improvement. We always end with a critique by some one member, and that seems to me to be a good plan.

"Altogether, our boys speak well, and are improving rapidly. It is far better than cards or mere talk. We debate some three times a week."

This practice Sergeant T. kept up after

the mess above referred to was disbanded, and the non-commissioned officers were distributed into tents with the men.

Indeed it was under this arrangement, in a Sibley tent with twelve privates, that he best showed his aptitude for a soldier's life. His habits of cleanliness and neatness led him to insist upon the daily use of washtowel, comb, and tooth-brush for the person, as much as upon oil and emery for the gun. His ingenuity devised many contrivances for the compact and orderly arrangement of equipage and utensils, and multiplied the comforts and enjoyments of the men. Said one of them, himself a mechanic, "The sergeant was always proposing some new ideas for our comfort; he would draw a plan, and teach us how to make this and that [pointing to various racks, etc. in the tent], so that he cared for us like a brother." Said another, "We used to watch for him to come in, he had such a pleasant way with him; he always had a kind word for every one in the tent." And they all testified, "In all the time he was with us, we never knew him to get angry, we never heard from him an uncouth expression, nor saw in him any improper or ungentlemanly action."

To divert the men from cards, he proposed making a set of chess-men, a large part of which he carved with his own knife. His Sibley tent with thirteen inmates, poorly lighted by day or night, with a stove in the center occupying the place of a table, afforded much smaller accommodations for reading and writing than the old wall tent for five. But he maintained in it order, comfort, and good cheer.

"We play chess a good deal now, having made a set of men and a board. It is very pleasant, and a good change from whist or euchre. We have a rule to stop all games if any quarrel arises, as sometimes cannot well be avoided;—I mean a quarrel in words, but this is not at all frequent."

He kept up as much as possible his own literary habits and tastes. His daily mail usually exceeded that of any one in the regiment. As he was well supplied with books and newspapers, Tent No. 4 became the circulating library of the company.

His boxes of creature-comforts sent from home, were shared with his tent-mates as freely as if they had been mess-officers.

"This is our Christmas eve, and yours, too. To-day my box came, and it was equal to any one of Professor Hermann's performances to unpack it, and reveal article after article till my whole bunk was covered, and then to end by removing a whole library from the bottom—all from one wee box. Everything was in prime order; it could not have been opened for inspection; and to repack it—why, I could only lay back half of the things! The books are just the ones for Tent No. 4. We shall spend much time in reading; indeed we are already at work. The drawing materials are all useful, and I will improve, if I can." By help of the timely box, and a few extra purchases from a distant farm-house, the Christmas festival was kept with even greater gusto than around the well-spread family board. The tent dinner was served upon the top of his bunk, which was covered with newspapers in lieu of a cloth.

" Of course we did not eat in silence, but joke followed joke, and we had a jovial old time. *No liquor* on the table. After our dinner was over, we called on one another for toasts and speeches, as we sat around the stove smoking our cigars and pipes, and those at home were by no means forgotten. I consulted my album, to see how you all looked. Altogether, we had a very merry time."

In the same cheerful vein he writes to a sister : " I hope you will enjoy the skating, though we don't want much more cold here ; for when the wind blows and rattles the tent as though it would pull it up, and it is freezing cold, then I think a brick house and a good furnace, with Bridget to put on the coal, might be warmer ; but I don't believe that any brick house contains a nicer family of thirteen than you might find in our white tent of an evening. It is so cold to-night that I can hardly write; it rains outside, and is dreary, cold. Of course I think of you all at home, but I do not feel home-sick at all. I am too much in for it now.

"We are very cozy in our quarters. My men have built me a fine bunk. In place of a feather bed, I have two thicknesses of newspaper on the boards! I sleep very soundly, and am never troubled with lameness."

While he was thus contented and cheery in his personal feelings, he studied to allay discontent among others, and also to remove its causes. After a serious sickness, he writes:

"I can only lay my illness to poor cooking, half-cooked beans, and once our meat was tainted a little. It is a shame that when Uncle Sam gives us such abundant rations, and of good quality, we have them ruined by the cooks. I am doing all in my power to have more care given to these matters, but cannot say much; for a sergeant should set a good example to the men by not grumbling."

XVIII.

HIS Christian character was never demonstrative. With him religion did not run much to the tongue. To his parents, indeed, he had sometimes unveiled the recesses of his soul-life with a freedom that he would use with no others ; and his very questionings concerning points of personal experience, and his conflicts with innermost temptations, were both in manner and in subject-matter imperative evidences of his sincere and principled piety.

In illustration of the prayerful habit of his mind, the following paragraph from a composition upon early friendships, written while he was a member of Phillips Academy, is here appropriate :

"While we are choosing from our com-

panions those best adapted both to sympathize and to rejoice with us, let us not forget that there is a Friend above all others,
with whom a true friendship may and should
be formed by all. Knowing that this friendship is purer, more beautiful and lasting
than any that can be formed with earthly
friends, that this love is without height or
depth—unchanged as the long ages of eternity roll on—forget not thy Creator in the
days of thy youth."

He had learned to trust in Jesus as a
Friend. I see him now, as he stood with
me alone in his chamber strapping his knapsack for his journey to Wheeling—the parting interview. The day had been given to
his outfit. "Well, John," I said, "I believe
I have procured everything that you will
need. But there is one thing that you alone
can care for. You are going upon a very
serious business, with temptations and dangers, perhaps sickness and death before you.
You must keep near to Christ, my son, in
prayer; never forget that."

Pausing for a moment in his preparations, he turned his large loving eyes full upon me, looked his whole soul into mine, and answered, " Father, *I think I'm all right there.*" His religious habit was so reticent, so thoughtful, so sincere, that those few words expressed to me his whole inner life.

The well-thumbed Testament and knapsack manual for devotion, among his effects, bear witness to his fidelity in keeping himself "all right there ;" and the testimony borne by all to the pureness of his speech and manners, and to the Christian elevation of his whole life, proves how thoroughly he was right within.

He deeply deplored the lack of a proper religious element in the organization of the regiment. Alluding to the ordination of a chaplain in the Broadway Tabernacle Church, he writes to his father :

"I hope in your charge to the chaplain you gave him some good advice. Ours is a Universalist, and I do not think much of him. As far as I can see he does not under-

stand the duties of a minister, for what is a
chaplain but a minister, and the regiment
his congregation?   If he has a meeting on
Sunday and one on Wednesday, and attends
to a funeral once a week, is he doing his
duty as a *Christian?*

"There is an immense amount of work for
a minister in our regiment ; of course I don't
mean simply work to convert or make a
Christian of every man, but work to check
profaneness, vulgarity, gambling, intemper-
ance, though of the last two there is very
little.

"I wish we had a man of good sense and
real interest in his calling. Our chaplain is
kind enough ;—by chance I know him, and
since my sickness he inquires for my state
of health ;—but speak to the men, to put in
a good word in a pleasant and appropriate
manner, never—in our company at least."

Again he makes this memorandum with
regard to religious privations in the camp.

"One of the worst evils of the army is the
loss of the Sabbath day. To-day I have

worked harder than I ever did on a week day at home. The men have been complaining for some days of want of full rations, good cooking, etc. Our rations are drawn for five days, except bread and meat which come daily. Last evening the Captain decided to divide the company into four messes of twenty-four each. So all last evening we worked (*we* sergeants) till eleven, forming the messes, and only seemed to make worse messes of the whole. Then this Sunday morning we worked until inspection at nine, in dealing out rations, drawing for pots and pans, etc. ; and then after inspection till two o'clock forming the messes and dealing rations.

" As for Sunday services, our chaplain is a Universalist, and I never go to any of his preachings. I think a service is rare, however, not more than once a week, if that. I am very sorry that he happens to be of that persuasion ; it is quite a loss to me, and he does our men no good. But this can only be laid to the account of privations and losses

12

suffered by the soldier." This chaplain soon resigned his post.

In minor morals the sergeant maintained a proper walk amid all the temptations to laxity which abound in camp life. He made decency of speech and deportment indispensable to a personal friendship. He did relapse, however, into the use of tobacco ; and in writing jocosely to his father to purchase him cigars of a certain brand, he says :

"I shall not argue the tobacco question, because we both agree to a great extent ; but you are not in camp. I will urge nothing in its favor ; simply saying that if smoke one does, certainly the better the tobacco the better for the smoker ; and nothing extra can be obtained in Virginia—only poor stuff, at sutlers' prices."

Not wishing, however, to burden the paternal conscience with complicity in this indulgence, he insisted that it should be charged to his private account! Indeed, he was minutely exact in his personal expenses ; careful to avoid debts or pecuniary obligations to others ; prompt and honorable in meeting his dues for camp extras, and thoughtful and liberal in remembering the birth-days and festal-days at home, by remittances from his slender wages. The very last line he wrote was in acknowledgment of a box of groceries and a remittance of postage currency. Learning that all his own remittances had been deposited in bank to his credit, he says : " I do not like to use money of yours. But you have the advantage of me. Only promise that if ever you are ' short,' you will draw on me." He that is faithful in that which is least, is faithful also in much.

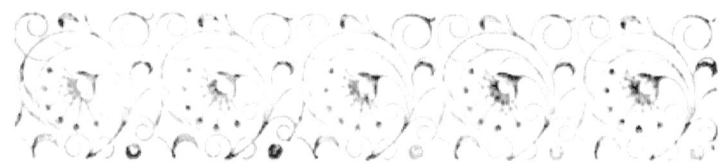

XIX.

THE sergeant had a soldier's ambition to prove his sword. "Our Colonel is a college graduate, perfect in drill and ability to teach others. I am in Company A, the first in rank and material. And although an entire stranger at first, I think now that I have many good friends. Though I have done no fighting, yet is it not share and share alike to those who fight and those guarding the stuff? We *may* fight yet .... I am quite contented and never for a moment regret enlisting."

His letters uniformly breathe this spirit of personal contentment, with a burning zeal for more vigorous action. He writes to a

sister : " I should like to go to some of the
Philharmonics this winter ;—but I don't
care, I want to see an end to this war before
I attend to music, or at least to see some
service. At present, our brass band and
drum corps satisfy me."

" The wind, rain and hail last night, did
some damage to our tent, by pulling up tent
pins, etc. The tent nearly came down, and
the wind whistled in and out all night ; but
we had a jolly time putting things to rights
and making all secure. We have no stoves
as yet ; and during the clear moonlight
nights we should freeze, were it not for our
overcoats and blankets. I was fortunate
in drawing a very heavy blanket worth
two like the old 22d.

" We shall be glad when we are fairly in
our winter quarters and have our stoves.

" But I am enjoying myself and am not
sorry at all that I enlisted. Those who are
at home in warm houses with every luxury,
or even plain comforts, do not know at all
how rough camp life is. Whenever you can

12*

do anything for any part of the army, don't begrudge it. Don't let the church hold back lest labor should be wasted.

"But I must not write so, lest you should think me home-sick, when I am not."

As weeks wore away in camp at New Creek, he grew more and more impatient for an active participation in the war; and like many a private soldier, he seemed to have a better grasp of the situation than some commanding generals.

"As to war and politics, I am glad that little 'Rapid'* is so fairly squelched. Give us leaders that will fight; we want men to march us on, to Richmond. For the love of country, don't make our great and noble army guard railroads. Regiments spoil for want of work. All our boys want to advance, fight, end the war and return home. And this is so everywhere. We all need fighting officers. Within a week this post has been thoroughly reinforced. Last week

---

* An army nickname given on the principle *Lucus a non lucendo.*

we had but about a 3,500 force, to-day nearly 12,000. These are mainly from Ohio and Virginia, ours being the only N. Y. S. V. We have artillery, three batteries; cavalry, a battalion and two companies; infantry, ten regiments, and more coming. Besides this, a very good fort nearly completed. So this place is well occupied. You can hardly imagine the *life* of so many camps.

"This morning I went as sergeant of the day, with Capt. P., officer of the day, to visit the pickets, taking the countersign and various instructions. We rode in four hours, including stops, upwards of twenty miles, which on these roads and by-paths is pretty good; you would have thought so, had you seen us gallop; spurs. in to the hub and horses on a dead run wherever the road would in any way permit. P. is the old one himself to ride, and I kept close to him: his horse was used up, and mine lost a shoe before we returned to dinner. For this afternoon we have fourteen miles more to visit pickets, and then every camp in place must be inspected. To-night every picket must be visited again, making upwards of seventy miles riding. All this is daily attended to by some officer in turn."

This was a sketch of army life addressed to a classmate at Yale. In a home-letter of about the same date, he says :

" If any of you thought we had hard times and made sacrifices last summer, what would you say now ? I have had far harder times than the hardest in the 22d, and am still far from the worst. But I expected it, and can stand more, if we can only do some good ; but this everlasting guarding of the railroad in a rebel state is a humbug. Why not make ours the fighting and the Southern the guarding army ? What is the use of making this rebel road our base of operations, and keeping 25,000 men to guard it ? Let the secesh destroy the road, if Maryland can't defend it. Let our *army* go to Richmond, let us form a line of operations from East Tennessee to Port Royal, only 200 miles, and fight them on both sides. Let the Home

Guards protect home and railroads. We are tired of guard-duty."

This guard-duty, however, was not always a quiet routine.

" By telegraph from Gen. Kelly we are under orders to be ready at a moment to march or fight. All may be mere false alarms, or we may soon fight here or near Cumberland. The regiment is ' spoiling for a fight' and will, I think, fight well. Our men have left their farms and business to come and put an end to this war and then go home to live in peace ; and when the time comes to strike a blow, it will be a ' mighty hard one,' as the boys say."

This alarm was succeeded by a brush with Imboden, in which a part of the 106th were engaged.

" On Saturday a force consisting of cavalry and artillery and Mulligan's infantry went out to attend to some rebels. Fifty-six miles from camp they found some eight hundred secesh. These drew up in the valley or pass, and seemed determined to stand. A few shells routed them, but the fight lasted about four hours. The rebels gave us several volleys and then the shells drove them to the hills, and as they ran up the mountains our guns were depressed even till holes were dug to sink the trails. We killed some forty or fifty, captured nearly forty—brought in to Cumberland—and took four hundred hogs and some cattle, all safely brought in. Our loss only three wounded."

Such turnouts, he writes, "frighten some, and excite others, and do good to all. If we could only have an advance, and put an end to Stonewall!"

That this was not mere boyish bravado, is evident from the deliberation with which he had counted the cost. In a familiar journal to a sister, he incidentally reveals his forecasting of death:

"There is a funeral just starting from Col. Mulligan's regiment. I hear the muffled drum beating in slow time; poor fellow! it must be hard to die of sickness in this country. But some must die in camp of fevers, etc., some must die fighting, and some will return home. But then I thought of all this before I started, and I hope I am willing and ready for either."

This preparation for death was exemplified in the minutest details of his personal affairs. On the fly-leaf of his Testament, his memorandum book, and of other knapsack treasures, he had written, "To be returned to 32 W. 36th street, New York"—thus anticipating a sudden death by addressing mementoes to his friends, that even a foe would respect.

It was not his way to repeat himself in his letters, nor to multiply words upon any subject. When he had settled his own convictions of duty, he would express them once for all, and abide by them. And perhaps the most solemn and weighty determination of his life would be uttered as a mere "aside," in some familar letter or talk with a friend, dropping from him as a matter of course. And so it happens that his most comprehensive and decisive judg-

ment with regard to the war, is found in a
frolicsome letter to a college classmate,
whom he addresses as his "dear Chalk."
Alluding to his three years' enlistment, he
says, "So Chalk, you may give it out as
rather improbable whether I return to College. Remember me to the class, and at
your next Delta Kappa meeting, as one who
thinks it his duty and the duty of every
man to go and *fight* in this time of need.
And more particularly the duty of such as
you are, who have good habits formed, and
are ready and quick to learn—that intelli-
gence and refinement may prevail in our
army, and that it may not be left to the
scum and scourings of the land to win the
battles and claim the laurels. Every one
of us ought to say in future years, 'I used
that gun in '62, '63,—or better, that *sword!*'

"I know we want education; but where
is the good of education without your country? And where is your country without
your men to fight and make it?"

A friend to whom this sentiment was sent

as an index of the sergeant's character, thus responds :

"My dear and bereaved friend ; That is a noble passage in the letter of *our* youth. Is he not ours—mine? Has he not laid down his life for my country?* I sympathize most deeply with you, more so, perhaps, than any other person out of your immediate family. These things come home with me.

"There is no other comfort to be offered to you—and can there be greater comfort? —than that he died young in a great cause, and that he died trusting in his God. It is in life as it is in science, in art, and in religion—in moments, actions, sufferings and speculations of the last importance and intensest energy, we must always recur to the first and elementary truths, to the simplest facts. It is so when we lose our first born. Of what unspeakable magnitude is then the truth that we shall see one another

* Though Professor Lieber is a German, no one has done more than he to vindicate our nationality, and to rally his countrymen for its defense.

13

again, and shall see one another forever
after a brief space! I know very well that
this does not dry tears—why should they
be dried? but it comforts the soul. Death
has long appeared to me but a mere question, by what train we or our friends go.
We are all going the same way and shall
soon meet again, though one goes by an
early train another by a later one. But
are not all of us standing and waiting at
the station?

" God comfort you.

" Very truly your fellow mourner,

" FRANCIS LIEBER."

XX.

"Man proposes and Stonewall Jackson disposes; so who can tell what will happen?" It was thus that the Sergeant announced to a college chum his "change of base." A hurried line of Dec. 27, announced "marching orders," and a few days later he hails from Martinsburg, in good health, "well acclimated by a summer and a winter in Virginia," full of pluck, and eager for work.

"Yesterday I was on duty at the Provost guard. We had thirty-six rebel prisoners to guard, beside the drunken men of the town. These rebels are a smart set, and require close watching. This morning two of them got into a fight, and I had to 'fall in' to stop them. I thought at first there would be a general fight, in which case about six of them would have been shot by my revolver pretty quickly ; but I managed to fling the two apart and to quiet them down."

The winter wears away at Martinsburg much as the fall had done at New Creek ; the same routine of duties,—only the picket service more arduous by reason of distance and the weather,— the same occasional alarms, the same eagerness for some decisive movement.

"There is almost no news at all, nothing but muddy weather, rain, and thaw. If the troops at Fredericksburg have such weather, don't blame them for not advancing. I do wish that the men by whom the pontoon trains were delayed might be shot ; and also, that Mr. Lincoln and his Cabinet would attend to their own business, see that we are punctually paid, and leave the *fighting* —when, how, and where—to our leaders. How could you in your study, by the advice of your deacons, direct the movements of this regiment? or say to our colonel when, where, and how he shall drill? It is just as absurd for Lincoln to dictate to Burnside. And why is General Butler recalled?

"It is the universal testimony of every man here, every Union man, that at Antietam the rebels were whipped out, and as they retreated here, they were disorganized and expecting to be followed up and cut to pieces. But McClellan must wait, wait, wait. In short, we are tired of such warfare."

One solace, however, never failed him— his home correspondence kept up against every disadvantage. To his mother who had praised him for his fidelity, he says:

"Thank you for your compliment in last evening's letter. I do not know how I deserve it, for I write my letters very rapidly, in a tent full;—there were nine here when I commenced this,—(tent, ten feet by ten) and rarely have time to read them over. But I like to write, and to write home; indeed I do but little other writing.

13*

"I do not think you need to feel at all anxious about me, for if I am sick I always write and can telegraph at any time. In case of a fight—well, you have an account of our last battle, and our future fights this winter will probably be the same. Besides, I came to fight and do any thing in the love of country line, even to camploafing."

Almost every day brought its own incidents, sometimes its special lessons of fact or principle.

"On Friday, I was on picket on the Winchester road. Two blacks came with a four-horse wagon, one a young man of twenty-five years, the other a man of fifty. They stopped to show their passes, and the old man jumped out of the wagon to light his pipe by our fire.

"Are you a free man? I asked.

"'Yes, sir, I paid a thousand dollars for myself, then I bought my daughter and my wife.'

"Well that was bully for you—but what

did you want to buy yourself for? didn't
you have a kind master?

"The old man took his pipe from his
mouth and looked at me.

"'*No slave ever had a kind master*, sir.
You get a little bird and put him in a cage
and feed him and take care of him and all
that, but you open the door and away he go ;
he know.'

"I told him he was well worth a thousand
dollars. Why is this county excepted in
Lincoln's proclamation?"

In February he begins to feel the severity
of the season—"It is very cold. We pile
on the wood, but with almost no good
effect, and I 'enjoy' a severe cough and cold.
But I shall get over this sometime, I suppose. Snow again this morning—fast and
cold. This is a hard time for pickets,
standing out all day in the snow and storm,
and then all night too, with only an open
fire. . . . We drilled yesterday for two
hours in snow a foot deep."

These exposures laid the foundation of

his fatal disease; and it is now evident that during February his health was seriously impaired. Yet so cheerful was the tone of his letters that not a suspicion of danger was awakened in the minds of his friends.

Alluding to the death of young Lieutenant Gray,* he says, " I am sorry for any one dying of fever or other camp sickness. We all regard such deaths as to no purpose, and I am sure many have died in this regiment when good home care would have saved their lives easily. But the Government is so slow to give a furlough or discharge, as a precaution for its own interests against fraud, that often before the leave to go home arrives, the poor sick soldier is only waiting for his final home. I would not complain, indeed I cannot be too thank-

* Lieutenant *William Cullen Bryant Gray*, of my own flock, a thorough officer, a promising scholar, a devoted Christian— o having passed through the battles and exposures of General Pope's campaign in Virginia, as an officer of General Doubleday's staff, died in a hospital at Washington, of a fever contracted while directing an engineering corps on the Rappahannock.

ful that we have had so few hardships. I will reserve all trouble for harder times than these. Suppose we were ordered to march to-night, and kept moving for weeks without a tent to cover us? or sent on picket where no fires were allowed? or forced to work in swamps and woods building bridges and earthworks? It may all come, but as yet I have seen but few hardships. However, we are undergoing a steady toughening process, four hours' drill daily, and guard duty about every five days."

On the 1st of March, 1863, he wrote to his mother, "I think I am now on the straight and narrow road that in this camp leads to health. After all forms of coughs and colds, sore lungs, side-ache, face-ache, tooth-ache, ear-ache, head-ache, neuralgia, fever, starvation (what's pork and dry bread to a sick man?) I am still alive and trying hard to keep so. Two days, Thursday and Friday, I spent in a hotel, but returned to camp in perfect disgust, preferring the comforts of a Sibley tent to any bar-room in

Martinsburg. I only want now my box as sent for, to 'set me up.' The amount of it all is, that I have had a pretty long sick spell and now am much better, though cough and cold still cling to me.

"It is very muddy here, but a strong wind blows, almost enough to take the tent over. There has been some trouble below Winchester, and a fight is somewhat expected. All the people here expect Jackson to return, and I should not be in the least surprised if he did, some time in the spring, just to season the 106th."

Five days after, the regiment removed to North Mountain—"A hard march of ten miles, in mud and water;—a hard one for me at least, as I was not fully in strength; but it did me good, I am sure." This (of March 7th) was his last letter.

His captain and the surgeon had attempted to dissuade him from marching; but he insisted that he would go with his men. The men endeavored to relieve him of his knapsack, but he insisted that a sergeant should set a good example to privates. "I never saw," said one of them, "such courage and energy as the sergeant showed. We all thought he was not equal to the march; but he would not be relieved. He said that he must be a *soldier*, and do all his duty for his country."

He had just been advised that his promotion to a lieutenancy was determined upon by the Colonel—"Well," said he to his informant, "if a commission comes to me, of course I shall not object; but I do not aspire to it." And to another he remarked, that "he had enlisted with a determination to do anything for his country; and he sometimes felt that he could serve it better as he was, than in some higher office, with more temptations to consult his own case."

On the day after the weary march to North Mountain, he insisted upon taking his regular turn on picket duty, and for this purpose went out several miles from camp. A snow-storm came up in which he passed the night. The next morning, Monday, he barely dragged himself back to camp, and sank down in his tent with severe symptoms of typhoid pneumonia. The surgeon was absent, and there was no hospital. But after two days he was removed in an ambulance to a private house, where he lingered until the night of the following Sabbath.

The kind friends who waited on him there found him "so gentle, patient, and uncomplaining in his spirit, and so delicate and sensitive in his habits, that it was almost impossible to render him any service. And at the same time he was so composed and resolute, so cheerful and hopeful, that it was difficult to realize how sick he was."

A pious captain visited him for the sake of religious conversation, knowing nothing of him personally. "I soon perceived," he says, "that I was talking with one who was no stranger to these things, and found him entirely at peace with God."

Two of his tent-mates watched over him with brotherly fidelity, and one of them reports from written memoranda the closing scene.

"About 11 P. M. the doctor called to see him; his breathing was very irregular. The doctor shook his head, as much as to say the case was hopeless. It seemed that the sergeant for the first time fully realized his danger. He asked the doctor if he could stand under it; the doctor told him he could not. He then asked if it would not be well to telegraph to his father. He was told that the captain had already done so. He expressed his satisfaction, adding, 'I am so glad; father will be sure to come to-morrow.' He then looked me full in the face and grasped my hand and said (calling my given and surname), Good-bye. A cold shudder went through my frame, as it was the first time I had ever stood face to face with death. He still held my hand and said, 'Send my love to my dear father and mother, brothers and sisters. I hope to meet them in heaven.' He made a few requests concerning his personal effects, then prayed to

14

God to forgive him his sins. After two or three short prayers, he asked Tanner to sing. He sang as well as his voice would permit, a verse commencing, 'Asleep in Jesus, blessed sleep.'

"When he had finished, the Sergeant requested him to repeat it, which he did with more composure. He then asked some one to pray—but neither of us had ever made a prayer; and were silent. He made the request again, but neither of us could say a word. He then prayed again himself. The captain came in soon after and tried to revive him—but he kept gradually sinking until about a quarter past one, when he settled into a composure or ease, and breathed more regular but shorter, until his breath entirely left him at 1.30 A. M., March 16th, 1863."

Servant of God, well done! *
  Rest from thy loved employ:
The battle fought, the victory won,
  Enter thy Master's joy.

At midnight came the cry,
  "To meet thy God prepare!"
He woke—and caught his Captain's eye;
  Then, strong in faith and prayer,

His spirit with a bound
  Left its encumbering clay;
His tent, at sunrise, on the ground
  A darkened ruin lay.

Soldier of Christ, well done!
  Praise be thy new employ;
And while eternal ages run,
  Rest in thy Saviour's joy.

XXI.

HE "died in camp of fever"—the death he least desired ; and I realized what it was to "hear the muffled drum beating in slow time," as I followed him from the chamber of death to the train that would bear him homeward. At the station in Baltimore a soldier inquired whose remains I was guarding. On being told, he exclaimed, "Why the 106th is my regiment, and I knew Sergeant Thompson, though he was not in my company. I remember his passing my picket with that rebel captain. How he put him through ! Yes, Sergeant Thompson ; he was always quiet and gentle ; looked as if he couldn't stand it, he was so slim ; never said much, but *always did it*."

Beautiful and touching was the tribute paid to the young soldier at the funeral solemnities in the Tabernacle Church : by comrades in arms from the 22d regiment, by classmates from Yale College, by the young men of the church, its officers, and the congregation at large ; very precious, comforting, elevating were the utterances, in prayer and address, of the beloved brethren who led the thoughts and devotions of the assembly.* Serene as peace after victory,—the mournful cost forgotten in the exceeding great reward—was the impression of the closing hymn, the departed soldier smiling, in the holy calm of death, with his sword beside him :—

> Thine armor is divine—
> Thy feet with vict'ry shod ;
> And on thy head shall quickly shine
> The diadem of God.

---

* Rev. W. I. Budington, D. D., of Brooklyn, conducted the devotional service ; Rev. R. S. Storrs, D. D., of Brooklyn, delivered an address of remarkable richness and force, which will be found at the close of the volume, as kindly written out from his own memory, after the loss of a phonographer's report. The musical

"The flowers were lovely," said one, "the music was tender and impressive, but the sight of that worn and faded cap showing hard service, touched me more than all; I broke down at that."

"His countenance to me," said another,[*] "was full of holy inspiration as it lay so calmly beneath the flowers and sword of death. I remembered him as I used to see him at Andover, with his noble, gentle ways. I shall always associate his character with the heavenly ideal of Phil. iv. 8 : 'Whatsoever things are true, whatsoever things are honest, whatsoever things are just, whatsoever things are pure, whatsoever things are lovely, whatsoever things are of good report ; if there be any virtue, and if there be any praise, think on these things.'"

He was laid to rest with kindred dust in

selections consisted of the second movement, Allegretto, from Beethoven's Seventh Symphony, feelingly rendered upon the organ by Miss McGregor; and the Chorus No. 11, from Mendelssohn's St. Paul, "Oh, happy and blest are they that have endured," sung with exquisite pathos by the choir. Both organ and pulpit were draped with flags and festooned with flowers.

[*] Rev. J. M. Holmes, Jersey City

Greenwood. A Christian poet,* who knew what loves and hopes were buried with him, has woven this sonnet as a chaplet for his tomb :

𝔗𝔥𝔢 𝔆𝔥𝔯𝔦𝔰𝔱𝔦𝔞𝔫 𝔖𝔬𝔩𝔡𝔦𝔢𝔯'𝔰 𝔖𝔩𝔢𝔢𝔭.

Smile softly, skies! upon the grassy grave;
    Angels! about it holy vigils keep;
    Where calm reposes, in his dreamless sleep,
The young and manly, generous and brave:
Deck it, ye flowers that tears of love shall lave;
    Let faithful hearts full oft beat quicker there;
    A glory not of earth the spot shall wear:
For He, the Lord of Life, that died to save,
    Of the still sleeper saith—"*He is not dead!*
Whoso believeth, he shall NEVER DIE!"
    The mortal resteth here ; the immortal—sped
Swifter than wings or fleetest thought can fly
    Above yon burning stars—exults to climb
    Of Heaven's own life the eternal heights sublime!

* Rev. Ray Palmer, D. D., of Albany.

XXII.

IT was with a melancholy and yet a positive pleasure that I revisited, in May, the encampment of the One Hundred and Sixth at North Mountain. The regiment had received the "seasoning" for which the Sergeant had so often longed. They were just in from a hard fight at Philippi and Fairmount, having saved Grafton by a forced night march. It makes one feel the war, to go into a camp where all seem as sons or brothers, and hear the story of a ten days' campaign without tents or knapsacks—not a man had slept under a shelter, or changed his clothing—and, in the course of which, one circuit of near forty miles was made in two days, varied with four hours' hard fight-

ing. Some are left behind in rude but honored graves ; some are lying wounded in the
hospital ; some are prisoners : but these
worn, soiled, weary men are ready to go any
whither, to meet again the enemy they have
routed, and will fight on still for *my* liberty,
my government, my country. It is a small
thing one can do to thank them, to cheer
them, to send them little home-comforts, to
pray for them, to stand by them and the
good cause.

How grateful it was to gather up all the
pleasant memories of the departed, that
lingered in the camp and clustered especially
about tent No. 4. Indeed, it was not necessary to "gather" these, for they came in
upon every breath, as freshly as if he had
just been taken from his comrades.

"Our tent seems very lonely and sad : the
Sergeant was always so cheerful and lively,
we can't get used to being without him."

"He nursed me when I was sick ; gave me
his own bunk, and tended me like a brother.
I would have done anything for him."

"My place to lie in the tent was next the Sergeant; and, for many a night after he was gone, the sight of something that was his would make me feel so bad that I couldn't sleep. I had to get up, and go out and walk, for I couldn't bear to feel that he was gone. He was such a friend to us all."

" Everything in the tent reminds us of the Sergeant, and we try to keep things just as he placed them. Every one of us has some little memento of him. Mine is a picture that he used to value. I have sent it home to my brother, to be framed and hung up in the parlor. If I go back, I shall have it to remember the Sergeant as long as I live; and, if I don't get back, my brother will have it to remember us both by."

Ah! war is not wholly a school of the rougher passions. How much that is gentlest, purest, holiest in our nature is brought into consciousness by being brought into requisition, in the camp, the field, and the hospital.

Going again to Harper's Ferry, the scene of so many tragic changes, I was profoundly impressed with the desolating progress of the war.

The little engine house where John Brown extemporized his fort, looks no more formidable than when the brave captain was led out of it a prisoner. But the massive batteries frowning from every height—multiplied fourfold since Antietam,—mark the present guage of the war, that the blind impulse or the prophetic insight (I never could determine which) of one bold friend of the oppressed, here opened against the gigantic despotism of the South. Following his lead, as the condemned hero stooped to kiss a slave-child as he mounted the scaffold, so grim-visaged War here folds to its protection the emancipated bondmen of the valley. Not a slave remains, it is said, in all that county; few in all the region of the Shenandoah. And so the great sacrifices have their compensation. But nevertheless they are great sacrifices. One can measure them better by contrasts, at intervals, on such a spot as the Ferry, where the fury of the conflict has been so often concentrated.

There has been sad work hereabouts since last July. The desolation has been made three-fold more desolate, in the destruction of houses, fences, groves, and by the neglect of planting and sowing in the once fertile valley. Bolivar Heights and Maryland Heights are now both stripped of trees; and many a brown, dingy acre marks the site of a deserted camp. Saddest of all, here on this lovely slope where last summer I saw *my* regiment drill, I can count upwards of three hundred graves of soldiers, side by side, in unturfed rows, each with its rude wooden head-board with a number and a name. As I stoop to read, I have a tear for every one. Each grave represents wounded hearts far away, that have not had even the sad satisfaction of beholding the faces of their dead;—yet we cannot pause for private griefs in this great agony of the nation. Let who will die, if the nation lives. Let who will go mourning in the future, if from this dark and dreary night FREEDOM shall rise with new brightness and joy. And therefore I stand amid this camp of graves, and this appalling desolation, praising God that heroism is not dead, that virtue is not dead, that freedom is not dead, that my country is not dead; I bless God for every one of these who has given his life for the noblest cause of this or of any age; I adopt these stranger names as household treasures; and to parents, brothers, sisters, who gave up these and such as these, I would fain send out the All-hail of that grand Future which they have sown in tears and blood.

15

XXIII.

" A MAN that is in bitterness for his first-born " is a type of human grief that the pen of inspiration has characterized as calling for Divine pity. It were unjust to our own nature to attempt to suppress its strongest outgoings of affection; it were ungrateful to God not to confess our grief when he withdraws his most precious and most generous gifts. What such a gift is, they who have measured it from every point can yet hardly describe.

"I mourn and rejoice with you," says one,* "in the desolation of a large arena of earthly hope, in the assurance that not the grave but the bosom of Eternal Love has received

* Rev. A P. Peabody, D. D., Professor in Harvard University.

(170)

your child. I know—though the removal
was in infancy—what unutterable disap-
pointment there is in the death of a first-
born son. The two or three years for which
mine was with me, form a part of my life—
in its hopefulness, in its varied plans, in the
commenced realization of some of them for
the benefit of one in whom I was anticipating a posthumous earthly existence,—entirely unlike the time before and since ; and
I can well understand and deeply feel,
how all this must have been intensified in
the twenty years of rich and beautiful promise for which your son was left in your
charge. God grant that we may both be
rendered, by such experience, the more meet
to renew our intercourse with the departed
in the Church of the first-born."

Another friend thus pictures the frustra-
tion of plans and hopes through such a loss :*

"There must be a thousand plans frus-
trated, some of which lay distinct in your

* Rev. E. A. Park, D. D., Professor in Andover Theological
Seminary.

own mind, but the greater part of which had not been brought out into your own distinct consciousness; yet all of which had more or less secretly influenced your life, and cheered you amid your many toils. How many visions a father has of his own plans out-reaching his own life, and given over to his son, to be carried out long after the father has been in the land of silence! And how well fitted a son is to finish what his father has begun! What a blessing Charles Francis Adams is to the world, in preserving so many memories of his father and grand-father, and giving to his country a better view of its true mission than could be given by any man who had not access to the private papers of the two Adamses! And I do not doubt that you have had, and will have a hundred projects which your son might have carried forward better than any other man could have carried forward.

"But why dwell on such disappointments? I do not know why. It is well for a man to feel his whole trouble. No one but yourself can possibly know how heavy your loss is ; but the heavier it is, so much the dearer is the thought that God understandeth all things, and He has made a greater gain than you have suffered loss. And if the Lord is the gainer, then may his children well afford to be losers ; for their loss is but for a moment, and is soon swallowed up in His gain, which is infinite."

One to whom I, in common with the whole Church of Christ, owe grateful honors for the Christian and heroic training of his first-born, and tearful thanks for his record of " the Child of Prayer," gives this kindred sympathy :

" I condole with you with the utmost sincerity, *non ignarus mali.*

" The Lord was gracious to you in the character of your son. And his departure, though painful in many of its attendants, was not without compensating facts of pensive and mellowing interest. To stand thus rooted in the vineyard and witness our branches cut off, one by one,—while our

15*

tears overflow, as the violated current of tender living sympathy between us and them,—can never be without distress. For myself such facts have made a living sorrow. But not long hence, the tree will also be removed—and we must live in anticipation and desire of that day. Bright and glorious it will be for those who love Jesus, I would fain hope even for me. I pray that our beloved Saviour may prosper your ministry and your household,—and make his purposes ever your delight."*

And closer yet, in the appreciation of certain aspects of such a loss, comes an honored guide of youth who first gave his son to die for the country, and then has caused him to live again a thousand fold in the story of his consecrated example :†

"How naturally and how deeply I sympathize with you, I need not say. We are *brothers* in this great affliction, as we seem

* Rev. S. H. Tyng, D. D.
† Rev. W. A. Stearns, D. D., President of Amherst College, whose touching memoir of his son, Adjutant Stearns, should be in every household in the land.

to be in the consolations which attend it. How much, my dear sir, there is to comfort us. Short but honorable were the lives of our precious boys. They have left a noble record, written in the nation's history on the hearts of their countrymen. They have gloriously 'fulfilled their course.' They have left hallowed memories for our sanctification, and the good of all who may hear of them. It is decided, and decided once for all, their lives were not failures. In Heaven before us—how pleasant when our turn comes, to think of going to meet them. We have been their teachers on earth, they will be our teachers in Heaven. We have helped them from our studies and experience to know the true God and Jesus Christ here ; they will help us by their higher spiritual wisdom and soul-ravishing happiness, to know them unspeakably better hereafter.

"These afflictions though they bow us down, I really think are tokens of an Infinite Love that sent them. Will they not enlarge our experience and enrich our lives ?

I think they will. A great sacrifice this, which we are called to make for our country. But oh! if the God of our fathers will only come and break the yokes of all the bondmen and remove the awful curse which is upon us, and save the nation, I shall say, *we* shall say, Amen, though the grave-clothes of our sons are winding-sheets of blood."

XXIV.

WE take up again that AMEN. The cause is worth the sacrifice; — worth infinitely more than any individual can do or suffer in its behalf.

"I do not undertake to say a word that shall look like condolence, or that shall have the aspect of grieving with you, or for you, for the death which is thus announced; for if I did, I am sure the language of your heart would be that of another under somewhat similar circumstances, 'I would not exchange the memory of my dead son for the possession of any living one that I know of.'

"How full, to the end of your life, of all that is grand, grateful, elevating and en-

nobling, will be thoughts and reminiscences
with which you and your family will dwell
upon the memory of what he was. No dark
spot in his life, no blight or blot on his
record, but all that a parent's heart could
wish, he died with a heart full of generous
sympathies, great aspirations for good, surrendering his life to the noblest of causes,
before experience had taught him aught of
the hollowness of earthly honor or the in-
gratitude of man.

"My friend, instead of condoling with
you on your loss, I congratulate you from
my heart on the priceless legacy which your
son was able to leave you : on the high
satisfaction, nay, on the honest pride, with
which you must always dwell on the memory
of such a son. And when this cruel war
shall be over, when a merciful God shall
restore our waste places, rebuild the temple
of our liberties, and our people renovated
and purified by that dreadful baptism of
blood and fire, through which we are now
passing, shall send to Heaven the grateful

thanksgiving of a regenerated nation, you shall feel an honest and an exultant pride in remembering how costly was the sacrifice you were called upon to make in procuring so great a boon.

"And when life's fitful scene draws to a close, I trust it will be among the most consolatory thoughts of a death-bed, that you are about to enter on a life, where not the least of its joys will be, that you are to join the Patriot and Christian son, whom you now mourn, never to be separated."*

Thus it was given to this soldier-boy by his death to strike anew the chord of Christian patriotism in many hearts, and to call forth utterances of lofty faith and heroism, for the times through which we are passing.

"Your account of that noble son," writes a consecrated leader in the cause of liberty, "fills me with emotion and inexpressible sympathy. But the thought of such a life, and such a death must be sweet to you—

* Hon. John P. Hale, U. S. Senate.

such an example will be a possession always." *

One who had known something of his
development since he first met him in London as a playful child, thus testifies :

"From what I saw of your beloved son
when we were travelers in Europe, I was
deeply impressed with the integrity, the
strength and the manliness of his character.
And when this wicked and terrible rebellion
broke out, I was not at all surprised to find
that he promptly offered himself for the
defence of our suffering country.

"It is an abiding conviction with me, that
great truths and principles are, for the most
part, established by great sacrifices. And
when such sacrifices as your noble son are freely laid upon the country's altar, I cannot doubt
that the reward will be found in the freedom, justice, and prosperity of the future."†

That is the exceeding great reward before all who labor and suffer for their coun-

* Hon. Charles Sumner, U. S. Senate.
† Rev. T. C. Upham, D. D., Professor in Bowdoin College.

try in these times; and no prayer has seemed to me more comforting than this from one whose name is largely identified with our grand uprising of patriotism. "May God comfort you, and yours, most graciously. And, above all, may He be pleased to give us, in this terrible struggle, our money's worth, and our blood's worth, in freedom and righteousness." *

That this blessed fruit will come, no heart that rightly believes in God's government of justice over this world, can permit itself to doubt. The very cost of the purchase is an earnest of the fulfillment. For, as writes a sagacious observer, "it is not the will of God that this rebellion should be overthrown, and with it the curse of slavery, without an enormous expenditure of precious blood as well as of treasure. But my faith is firm that the expense is well laid out, and will bring to our children a harvest an hundredfold."†

* Rev. R. D. Hitchcock, D. D., Professor in Union Theological Seminary.

† Rev. E. P. Barrows, D. D., Prof. in Andover Theo. Sem.

16

One whose faith rises almost to prescience, so grandly forecasts that harvest of good, that his prophecy evoked by a brief outline of the sergeant's career, seems like a resurrection of the dead.

"I have been much interested in this sketch of the life and death of your first born, a life in its morning promise and beauty, nobly laid on the altar of God and his country, and destined to bloom, yea, I am confident, already blooming in climes beyond the sun, and in a glory which shall not fade when fades the sun. A life, brief alas, to friends who loved and mourn, but yet in its true aspect as seen from the heights of the true universe, most rich, complete, and successful. For a life so pure, heroic, loving—inspired and ennobled by piety and patriotism and true to God and truth, even unto death—may be surely so denominated, however brief! A life baptized of God's spirit, devoted to a noble cause, surrendered at the behest of Right and Duty, and ending, short as was its limit, in the city of our God.

How much could earth or years add to a life like this? In our delusive time-ward and earth-ward vision, our mortal tears fall over such a career, so ending, as over something beautiful, but blighted untimely before fruitage. But the sons of God on the heights of the everlasting will hail it as a victory, a triumph, a glory. Of such it shall be written, these are they which loved not their lives even unto death, therefore do they stand before God, and serve him day and night in his temple.

"When I contemplate cases like that of your son, and think how many of the noblest and most gifted, the choicest and best of the land have fallen in the cause of the country, I am tempted to wonder, if not to murmur, and to ask why must such die? Why not be spared to the church, the country, and humanity? But it has been the law of noble causes ever in our world that they require the baptism of blood and tears—the best of the best. This is their lustration and conservation; their seal and signature in

history and to humanity. Our cause comes
under this law, and alas! it needs great
atonement.

" I know, my dear brother, that consider-
ations like these cannot staunch your tears
or beguile your heart of its bitterness for
the loss of your first-born. Nature claims
your tears and God pities them, and they
all fall in his sight. From our mortal stand-
point the grave is the goal, the limit of the
way. To the eye of sense the tomb-stone
hides for the bitter hour the shining city
which Faith sees in glory beyond. And
well I know that not all the eulogy and ac-
claim of loving and admiring friends—yea,
not even the joy of national victory and ju-
bilee can beguile the heart of its longing for
the loved form that shall never wake till the
resurrection morning. Long will the heart
ask for the first-born—the form that first
called you father ; the darling of your early
married life, endeared by the memory of
those beautiful years. Long will it ask for
the companion of your travel and your study;

the manly associate of your manly thought and counsels and commune. It will ask until you shall lie down in the dust beside him, and the grave shall open for you the way to the Eternal Reunion—a walk together under the shadow of that tree whose leaves shall heal all the woundings of our mortal life.

" But meantime there shall be comfort, at times, in thinking of the preciousness of what you have lost, and the cause and manner in which it has been lost, as well as of the certainty of its glorious restoration. And for that you ' have buried with him no small part of your life,' that which remains shall be richer, holier, happier ever—such is God's fullness—for this very loss : and shall partake on earth of something of the angel-boy that has gone before you to the skies. Affliction shall grow to glory, sorrow to a sweetness past all joy. For in the cloud and dark, the Lord himself shall descend and walk with the smitten one, and touch the earthly love of father and son with the sweetness and beauty, the holiness and the

16*

awe of the Divine and Eternal. That God
may bring you this blessedness from your
bitter grief, and by the gift of Himself infinitely compensate to you all earthly loss, is
the prayer of one in earnest and loving sympathy."*

* Rev. T. M. Post, D. D., St. Louis, Missouri.

XXV.

"DULCE *et decorum est pro patria mori.*
And for a Christian, I have often
thought there might be some special sweetness—if not, indeed, some unusual bestow-
ments of grace in dying, and some unwonted
cordiality of welcome after—in being permitted, in so close an imitation of the Saviour,
to *lay down one's life for others.* I cannot
help thinking that Jesus is very near to his
little ones when they die for their native
land; and especially when they make the
great sacrifice with so much of intelligent
comprehension of all the issues involved, as
your dear son evidently had grace to do.

"I congratulate you, my dear brother
that you have been found worthy of this

honor from the Lord : and I pray that you may
be made perfect through the suffering which
this honor brings.   And may the blood of
your young martyr—with that of the great
multitude who shared his trial and share his
immortality—be the seed of good things,
and great things, and glorious things, for
this land, and for Christ's church and for
God's world ;—things good and great and
glorious enough to pay for the lost seed ;
and that—though it lie buried long in the
dust !"*

"Such noble examples sanctify our cause,
and the griefs that accompany them purify
our hearts for a deeper and more effective
service in our Master's work.   Your great
loss has been a great gain to many others."†

"For all that displayed courage, persistence in the way of duty, high principle, just
sentiments and manly bearing, you have reason, great reason to cherish his memory and
bless God for having given you such a son.

* Rev. H. M. Dexter, Boston.
† Rev. H. W. Bellows, D. D., New York.

Nor, while you mourn, can you regret, that since he must die, he died in such a cause. Yet the true consolation to your spirit is, that to all his high manly qualities he added the faith and the graces of a Christian ; that his last hours were so sustained by divine hope ; and that you are permitted to indulge the undisturbed confidence that death has been gain !"*

" Nobly has your first-born met life's claims and filled up the measure of duty assigned him ; traversed his circuit without a mis-step, and now has gone to his reward. There let him rest. The separation will be short at the longest. His life and death will preach many a sermon to the living. I very much doubt whether the brave young Stearns would have done more for the world, had he lived twice as long, than he has done, *is* doing, and will do for how long a time none can tell !"†

" I do congratulate you that you had a son

* Rev. Thomas E. Vermilye, D. D., New York.
† Rev. Isaac P. Langworthy, Secretary of the American **Congregational** Union.

to offer and be offered, for his country's life ; and by all the traits which endear him to your memory, and by all the hopes which he relinquished, is the offering enhanced. He lived longer than his father has lived—compressing into his brief career of youthful patriotism and honor more of heroic achievement than is possible in the longest life, to any of us who, in the providence of God, are exempted from active service in the field on which are staked the issues of liberty and humanity, and the destiny of our dear native land. And when to the thought that he rests in a soldier's grave, numbered forever with the brave and faithful defenders of our country, is added the reflection that he sleeps in Jesus, awaiting with kindred and sainted dust an associated rising on the morning of the resurrection, I cannot but feel, my brother, that God has highly blessed you in your first-born."*

" You have all the comfort you could ask for in *such* a sacrifice as you have made.

* Rev. Samuel Wolcott, Cleveland, O.

And is it not of some worth, to be one of the 'exceeding great multitude' who have been counted worthy to make the sacrifice in this crisis? They seem to me a choice and bright assembly, if they have grace to bear the baptism they are baptized with."*

"I knew John," says a kinsman, "only as a lad of promise, and have seen him but little, but I deeply sympathize with you. It is the first time that this war has brought its melancholy side so heavily home to us. I will not attempt consolation ; you undoubtedly have it far better than I could give. I can only say that had I a son of my own, I should not have withheld him from the great cause in which we are engaged ; and if death had claimed him on the field, or in the ranks, it would have been some comfort in sorrow to feel that he died in defence of a principle more important than any previous contest in the world's history has involved."†

* Rev. Austin Phelps, D. D., Professor in Andover Theological Seminary.

† Dr. John K. Bartlett, Milwaukie, Wis.

An honored divine who made the boy his pet in travels on the Rhone, and in sight-seeing at Paris, writes :

"Ah! that dear noble boy; how can I feel grateful enough to God for having given you such a son. His bosom filled with noble sentiment, the soul of honor, truthfulness, courage, generosity, and yet undemonstrative, showing all based on prin-ciple ; and above all to have that character sanctified by the ever Blessed Spirit, the splendid temple laid in ruins by the first Adam, restored to much of its beauty by the second Adam,—of all this to have been made the recipient—what more can a father's heart ask ?"*

The head of a college that has nurtured Christian patriotism, and of a household in which the Sergeant's name was often spoken by those who had both known and loved him, writes :

"The event so full of sadness, has also another aspect of beauty and grandeur. It

_____
* Rev. J. H. Price, D. D., Rector of St. Stephen's, New York.

is a blessed thing to have had such a son. Very beautiful was the unfolding of Christian grace as he advanced in years and grew up to the stature of a man. Very precious are the memories of that brief life —almost unmarred it seems by any outbreak of waywardness, and the death which terminates that life is made grand by the self-devotion which in the coincidence of his own choice and God's appointment determined its time and place and manner. We could wish that it might have been prolonged, but the voice of God and of our common humanity declares it a noble life well ended,—no, not ended, but gloriously begun, through God's grace making death but the translation of the soul to the true sphere of its life. There with the welcome ' Well done, good and faithful servant,' he has already been ushered into the joys of his Lord and charged with more important trusts in His service.

"Then, too, as the event tests the sincerity and entireness of his sacrifice and yours, to

17

the cause of truth and humanity, so you may
rightly interpret it as setting the seal of
God's acceptance to the sacrifice.   And
what more could you desire? what more
could years of successful service bring?   All
was given—all is accepted—and in the end
it will appear that God has made the utmost
that he could of the child, the man so consecrated.   'Except a corn of wheat fall into
the ground and die, it abideth alone ; but if
it die, it bringeth forth much fruit,' applies
to the disciple as well as to the Master.
Your son has not thrown himself away.
His life has not been spent in vain.   Through
its sacrifice in the cause of righteousness, it
swells the measure of that suffering identified with Christ's suffering, which is at the
same time the purchase, price and the element of power for securing the world's
redemption from all evil.   From the little
seed thus sown, precious fruit will be growing,
and ripening through the ensuing ages."*

* Rev. A. L. Chapin, D. D., President of Beloit College, Wis-
consin.

This is the view that sanctifies and elevates our conflict; that invests our personal experiences of sorrow in this cause with something of that majestic import that pertains to the highest Christian sacrifice.

One who has devoted a life of self-sacrifice to laying the foundations of Christian institutions in Illinois, while looking back from the shadow of Oxford upon his western home, sends his estimate of the worth of our country, in these stirring words :

"I assure you that, looked back upon from England, my country seems infinitely precious. I do not know, for I have not yet been put to the trial, whether I have self-sacrifice enough to give my life, or give my son for any good cause ; but I am sure if I could make such a sacrifice for any thing, it would be for such a country as ours, in this hour of her calamity and danger. I see much to admire and love in England, but I never before saw so clearly what God has done for our country. With a full heart I thank the Lord that he sent my ancestors to America, six generations ago. I accept it, war and all, with all the uncertainties of the future.

"If by these terrible sacrifices our country is to be saved for a happy future of freedom and peace, then how you will rejoice that your noble son died not in vain; that by a death so early, and so honorable, he has done more for human well-being, than he could have done by the longest and most useful life." *

But the Gospel which inspirits our patriotism, imparts to these sacrifices a higher value, while it attends them with a richer consolation.

"I mourn with you, my dear brother, in your great sorrow to which you allude in a single line of your letter. May God help you to bear it, remembering Him who 'so loved the world that He gave *his* only begotten Son' for its sake. We are learning in this great strife how to understand God,

* Rev. J. M. Sturtevant, D. D., President of Illinois College.

and how to sympathize with him both in his justice and his mercy, in his wrath and his love. The cup of Gethsemane is put into our hands, the agony of Calvary is before us; but it is for the work of Redemption; without such dying of the just for the unjust there can be no remission.

"I know how the grave of that soldier-boy will seal your patriotism, and bring into it all the sacredness of your religion itself; how it will make it more impossible than it was before even, that you should ever cease to preach and to pray, to labor and to fight, if need be, until this bloody Moloch, which is devouring ten thousands of our sons, is hurled from his throne and driven from the land.

"My dear brother, may God mark your sacrifice in his book. May he give it its full place in that great and terrible ransom by which our deliverance is to be bought, and may you live to see the day when you can stand over that green grave and say, under the new light which shall then shine

17*

down from Heaven, the glory is greater
than the gloom, the reward is greater than
the sacrifice; I bless God that I had one
life to give for my country."*

* Rev. Leonard Swain, D. D., Providence, R. I.

XXVI.

BEAUTIFUL is the light of Christian faith and hope, when the evening of a long and useful life blends itself with the dawning of the life everlasting. This mellowed light of age, kindling anew with the advancing glow of immortality, turns its radiance back upon the grave of the young Christian soldier. The veterans of the school and the church pay their tribute to his faith and patriotism.

"Memorable is the record of the virtues, the heroic and high-principled patriotism, the noble spirit of self-sacrifice and religious devotion to the calls of duty, which impelled this brave and much-loved youth to encounter the toils, the fatigue, the privations and the dangers of war.

"In several visits with our friends at Cambridgeport, we were much interested in the unfolding character of your son, rich in promise and hope, but little did we dream that the cheering prospects of youth were to be eclipsed by the funeral-pall, even in the earliest years of opening manhood.

"It will not be long before the precious souls of our dear departed ones, who have been redeemed by our divine Saviour, will welcome their pious friends on their arrival in heaven ; and then, all the sorrows of this life will be remembered only as a part of Christian education for a better world.*

Another, whose name has been identified with the religious progress of the country, almost as long as that of Silliman with its progress in science, writes :

"Your account of the death of your dear son has just now reached me, in the midst of the storm, this last day of March. So there are *last* days of all months and years and centuries and of all the lives of men,

* Prof. B. Silliman, LL. D., Yale College.

excepting the life eternal, which is hid with Christ in God. To that no last day shall ever come. Begun in the life below, its temporary associations shall be changed, and its earthly ties severed, but it will not, cannot have an end. And the last days, on earth of those who inherit the life eternal through grace, are points of unutterable interest, to be remembered by all survivors, —sad, as " the *last* of earth," and still more sad when they terminate the lives of young persons nobly aspiring to goodness and usefulness, and the hopes and tender wishes of loving families are blasted in the bud. But joyful are these same *last* days, as seals, by the hand of God, of testimonies given, examples completed, and victories achieved ; more joyful still, as the *first* days of emancipation, the points of departure from sin and sorrow, upward and onward forever.

"You have seen and recorded the last day, and the last words of that dear son. You feel the loss of what he was, and of what he might have been to you and yours, and

surely you are in 'bitterness.' But, **my**
brother, happy is the parent who has such **a**
record to make, of **a** son so noble in his aspirations, and so **accordant**, heart to heart, **with**
himself. To have had the possession **and**
the training of such an offspring for such an
end, above all the sorrows of its loss, is **a**
joy forever." *

* Rev. Absalom Peters, D. D.

XXVII.

THEY who know what war is, know how to appreciate the death of the soldier in its relations to himself, to his friends, to his country.

"The *Congregationalist* of the 27th ult. brings to me the first intimation I have had that you are a personal sufferer by this war, in your own beloved family. I can't help writing you just a word to speak of my sympathy with you, and to record myself among the many, many friends whose eye will moisten at your grief as if it were their own.

"Familiarity with death on the battle-field and in the hospital has not made me less sensitive to the trying circumstances which

attend such a death, but more so. And
with a full knowledge of such bereavements
as we see them in the army, though without
any particular acquaintance with the facts
in this case, I heartily offer you my frater-
nal feeling, and pray my God to sustain and
comfort you.

"You are blessed, my brother, and favored of heaven in giving up your well-beloved
son to die for the nation, for the *age*, rather,
and those twenty years and six months of
earthly life, with such a termination, and
leaving behind so fragrant a memorial, are
worth more than any four-score years of ordinary existence. How fast we live now!
This may be the time the prophet had in
view in which 'the child should die an
hundred years old.' May our blessed Saviour be with you in this sorrow, and by it
touch your lips with a more tender and per-
suasive eloquence as you plead for the bond-
man whose dungeon door is just beginning
to open. You can hold nothing too dear,
not even your own life, to give for the coun-

try, for liberty, for Christian civilization, for God." *

And another voice from the field exclaims :

"How greatly has God afflicted you, and how greatly honored you! Happy they who can give so richly for the sacred cause of country and humanity. He too, your dear boy, is a part of *the great cost* at which the nation is to be redeemed. That is your precious, precious contribution to God's work in this land. By-and-by, we shall reckon up these priceless offerings. We shall recall and record these young heroic martyred names. One such sacrifice — in such a day — the whole consummate life thrown in at a single gift—there is no protracted service of late and many years that can peer it. How complete such a life and story. Nothing fragmentary and broken off here. White hairs and fourscore winters could not have so rounded and filled

* Rev. Horace James, Chaplain of the 25th Mass., and now Superintendent of the Freedmen in North Carolina.

out the earthly work. That young hand touched the crown and goal in life's morning. As truly as Paul the aged, could those boyish lips say, 'I have *finished* my course.' The nation will come presently and lay down the gratitude of its millions at such feet as yours—feet that walk more lonely from henceforth—and yet shall walk on the high places of a nation's honor and guerdon.

"God bless you, and comfort you, and reward you. I have my own first-born son with me in the 45th, our Colonel's mounted orderly. He has ridden safely thus far through all dangers. But I have given him to God and his country. He has, I believe, so given himself. I can feel something of what it would be to miss him from my side and from my home, henceforth—but he is God's — my offering is without reserve. These are days when life wins its ends early." *

* Rev. A. L. Stone, D. D., of Boston, now Chaplain of the 45th Mass.

XXVIII.

ONE who had some interest in the Sergeant when a school-boy at Cambridge, in speaking of "his noble and consecrated character," goes on to say, "the thought of the cause for which he died must do much to bear up a father's mourning heart. Sometimes I think of those who mourn as you mourn, and who make such sacrifices as you have made, as the privileged men of the land. But such sacrifices are very, very costly.'"

And my dear Oxford friend, the truest friend of America in England,* himself lying on the verge of death, shrinks back from the

* Mr. Joseph Warne, Postmaster at Oxford, whose personal influence and whose pen have widely and intelligently aided our cause.

demands of our cause, when told that the
boy he loved almost as his own had become
a sacrifice. " How vivid to me the young
student, the volunteer, the resolved whole-
war volunteer, the brave and courteous cus-
todian of the prisoner ;—and your own free
and forecasting surrender, and your comfort
and hope, in that he assured you all was
right Christ-ward. The dear Johnny of my
heart, so real ; so loved of my wife—you
hardly know how much she loved Johnny.
. . . . . Ah, the enormous cost of this contest,
not in money only but in the best life of the
country, quite dismays me. Your men are
too good for their work !"

And yet he feels also that the CAUSE dig-
nifies and elevates the sorrow and sanctifies
the loss. Rather would I rise to the tone
of him who having three living sons in the
service of the war, writes :

" Often since this great struggle began for
our country, and for liberty and righteousness, the regret has risen in my mind that
my eldest son, who died fifteen years ago

when he had just entered on his twenty-first year, could not have had the privilege of making the great sacrifice which so many are now making in the cause of our country, and of the world."

And such *is* the inspiration of Christian patriotism in every heart that measures the moral grandeur of our national struggle.

" As I came down from the pulpit yesterday," writes Rev. L. Pilatte,* " a friend handed me a newspaper addressed in your familiar hand. I opened it eagerly for news, when my eye rested on the sad announcement ;—your John, our dear Johnny was no more !

" The news was a blow to myself and my wife as if one of our sons had been struck. We remembered the lovely boy who had so endeared himself to us during his stay under our roof; we felt for you and with you. Sadness sat at our table that day, when we spoke of him and of you. Yet when I looked upon my three boys and asked myself how I

* Nice, France.

would have felt if one of them had fallen in
so noble a cause, I could not help thinking
that I would deem it an honor to have con-
tributed a son to its triumph. Of such sacrifices God makes the glory of his cause, and
the redemption of a people. But when
they multiply, when they come so near us,
we cannot help exclaiming, how long will
that dreadful conflict last? Not that I
would have it stopped on any account before
the rebellion is crushed and slavery with it;
but I watch with an anxious eye the slow-
ness of the North's movements, and I trem-
ble lest the people faint before the impious
power of the rebellion is annihilated. God
be with you and your armies! I have never
yet doubted even in the darkest hour the
ultimate success of the right among you.
Your bloody struggle, so long, so fearful,
will prove your salvation, and the initiation
of America into an era of undreamed after
greatness.

One who himself has known more than
thirty years of hardship, toil, sacrifice,

danger for the cause of Christ in a foreign land,—and whose son was the Sergeant's most intimate friend,—while sympathizing in " the great sorrow " that had fallen upon the household which was his home on his last visit to America, gives a missionary's estimate of our struggle in its relations to the kingdom of God.*

" In regard to the dear young man himself we have no reason to mourn. He is doubtless with Christ which is far better, and he could not have offered up his young life in a more just or noble cause, according to my judgment. To die in attempting to suppress the most audacious and wicked rebellion known to history is a high honor ; and whether successful or not, God will not forget the offering ; and in his own way and time, he will vindicate the memory of those who have thus sacrificed all in this sacred cause. If not to-day, yet it will not be long before this matter will be set right ; and

---

* Rev. W. M. Thomson, D. D., of the Syrian Mission, author of " The Land and the Book."

when the millions who fall in the vulgar
scramble after wealth will have been forgotten, those who shed their blood for law, liberty, truth and righteousness, will be held in
honor and everlasting remembrance.

" My recollections of your son are all very
pleasant ;—mild and amiable and conscientious, and self-distrusting, he must have entered the army from the very purest motives;
and I honor and reverence now, where I
merely admired and loved before. But alas!
for our country. It is just such instances as
this that enable me to realize the fearful
condition of things there, where all was
peace and prosperity when I left only four
years ago. Tremendous indeed must be the
pressure when such youth as I remember
John to have been, are roused and nerved
to face the grim front of war.

" And what is to be the retribution of
those gigantic sinners who have caused this
immeasurable mischief! But I need not
pursue this train of remark. Words are
very cheap. Were I in America, I would

be in the army, and act as well as pray and
preach. It is but little that any one man
can do, but that little I should most willingly
consecrate to the effort to suppress this most
monstrous slave rebellion."

Our country's noble and eloquent cham-
pion before Europe, mingles his tears of sympathy with words of lofty inspiration :

"*Au Rivage, 17th April*, 1863.

" My Dear Friend :—*How* to express to
you my deep and tender sympathy ! I have
cast myself upon my knees, I have besought
the Lord to multiply to you his aid. He
alone can speak to you what your poor torn
heart needs to hear.

" That dear young man ;—he has given
his life so purely and so nobly to a holy
cause ! In that brief career God has laid
upon him the fulfillment of a grand duty ;—
more than He often assigns to our long
course. And then, above all, that Christian
death ! Well do you know *where* to seek
him ! He has entered into the Father's

house, where the same grace of Christ has prepared a place for those who mourn him.

" And yet, it is well to weep—God does not condemn our tears. What a rending! I bewail you from the bottom of my heart. As your letter expresses it, 'a portion of yourself has been swallowed up in that dear tomb.' If it is sweet to you to know that other hearts are afflicted with yours, that hands reach forth from afar to clasp yours, that fervent prayers unite with yours, oh, be sure that this is so.

" You have recently had the great pleasure of seeing another of your children make a public profession of faith in the Saviour. Oh, that God would give us above all in our families the joy of feeling that we are one heart and one single soul for his service— that the word spoken to Paul might be addressed to us also, 'I have given thee all those who sail with thee.'

" It seems to me that your affairs take on a better aspect. Those internal dissensions that we had apprehended for you, do not appear to come to much. Maintain your unity. Bind yourselves around Mr. Lincoln.

" Adieu, dear sir and friend, I pray our good God to keep himself with you, to bless you, yours, and your dear country for which you have made so great and so mournful a sacrifice.

Receive especially my respectful regards.

A. DE GASPARIN.

XXIX.

THE Infinite Father opens avenues into his heart through the wounds that He inflicts upon our hearts, and interprets Himself to us through our personal experiences. Indeed God is often revealed to us through emotion where mere intellection would quite fail to apprehend Him. The sublime climax of divine love and promise is given in these few words : "He spared not his own Son."

At God's command Abraham took his Isaac, his delight, away from his home and his mother, to the mountain in the wilderness ; he laid him upon the wood ; he bound him with cords to the altar ; he made ready the knife—when the angel of the Lord cried " Forbear, lay not thine hand upon the lad."

He spared Abraham's son, but he did not spare his *own* son!

It may be that God calls you to Abraham's faith, and to more than Abraham's sacrifice; that he bids you lay your son upon the altar of patriotism, the altar of liberty, the altar of missions, the altar of humanity; and when the sacrifice is made ready, he sends no angel to stay it, he provides no lamb for substitution; he sees the blow about to fall, and lets it fall;—but when a horror of darkness, like that which encompassed Abraham, gathers about you, its folds are rent at the thickest; through your own riven heart, you look into the heart of the infinite Father; the glory of the Shekinah enwraps the sacrifice; and heavenly voices chant these words of love—*He that spared not his own Son will freely give you all things.*

It is not for human hearts to measure the love of God; it is not for human tongues to tell the love of God in Christ. We know not what heights of love they behold whose eyes death hath unsealed: we know not

what words of love they speak, whose
tongues death hath unloosed; but while
heart and tongue remain, we can know and
speak no greater love than these few words:

HE SPARED NOT HIS OWN SON.

XXX.

ADDRESS

OF REV. R. S. STORRS, JR., D. D., AT THE FUNERAL OF SERGEANT JOHN H. THOMPSON, IN THE BROADWAY TABERNACLE CHURCH, MARCH 20, 1863.

I AM not here, Brethren and Friends, to praise the dead. If I were otherwise moved to do so, the wishes of those whose wishes should of right control this occasion, would forbid my attempting it. We know too that *his* wishes, if once more his spirit could speak to us,—breaking for a moment the marble stillness that seals henceforth those silent lips—that his wishes, harmonious with those of his parents, would equally prohibit our words of praise. They are not

(219)

needed; certainly not in this place, and in this presence. You do not need them, his classmates and companions of the school and of college, who have come hither to look for the last time on the face that has been familiar to you, and to express by your attendance on these services your affection for his character, and your sorrow at his death. You do not need them, members of the Regiment with which he was connected when he first went forth to do battle for his country, and which he only left when its term of active service had expired, to join the other in which he died. You know for yourselves how faithful he was in every duty; how resolute, uncomplaining, and courageous; how full of soldierly spirit and patriotic devotion; and your presence here to-day attests your regard for him. Least of all is it needful that I speak in his praise to you, my Brethren, the members of this Church in which he was trained in the knowledge of God, and of the Gospel of Christ, through his unfolding youth; in which he made his public confession of faith in the Master, and consecrated himself to His service in the world. You know how true and tender he was; how manly and how modest. You have seen and noted his daily life, and have felt the impression of his conscientious and affectionate character. You have loved him, for his own sake, and for the sake of his parents. And you need no words in eulogy of him from my lips to-day.

Less, indeed, than at any other time, are such words needed here and now, as we stand before his coffin, and remember that his spirit will return to us no more. For it is one of the beautiful offices which Death accomplishes, to reveal to us more distinctly the excellence of the friend from whom we have by him been parted. We walk with such a friend, in the familiarity of life, without pausing to consider what it is in his character which makes him lovely or noble to us. But when Death has taken him, the memory, the sensibility, at once become ac-

19*

tive, representing to us more vividly than before the several elements, the various forces,
which were combined in his life to endear
him to us. Not that we do this with distinct and intentional logical analysis; but
that our thoughts, as inspired by our hearts,
do it spontaneously; until every mourner
finds it true that even as the sunshine,
streaming in through these windows, so
beautiful in itself, may be untwisted by man's
art into the various primary colors that are
braided together to make its perfect golden
radiance, so the separate excellences that
were blended and combined in the character
of a friend impress us individually, with
most distinctness, when we view that character through the prism of our tears.

No; it is not to praise the dead that I
have come hither, and am standing above
the coffin of him whom I remember in his
beautiful childhood—the coffin which you,
with affectionate hands, have heaped with
flowers, and on which you have laid the em-
blem of the Cross. I am here only to sug-

gest—as it seems to be meet that some one
should suggest—a few general thoughts
connected with the event by which we are
convened ; thoughts that are familiar, yet
that always are full of instruction and encouragement, and that hardly can fail to be
emphasized to us by the scene amid which
we are assembled.

The primary thought, and the most essential, of course, is that one which is always
impressed upon us anew whenever we con-
front the presence of Death : of the supreme
value that belongs to the Gospel ; the
entirely transcendent and incomparable
worth of a Christian hope. — Amid the
pleasures and excitements of life, the young,
especially, may not feel this. Religion to
them may seem a burden, not a privilege ;
and the prizes of life, as they glitter before
their ardent hope, may hide from their eyes
the heavenly splendor of the pearl of great
price. But here, to-day, as in every such
scene, we know and feel that the one thing
essential to man's well-being—the one thing

essential to the comfort of those who bow
in grief above the form of their unburied
dead—is the assurance of that faith in the
Master by which the grave is robbed of its
terrors; which makes it luminous with celes-
tial promises; yea, which enables us to
look through its portal, steep and narrow
as are the sides, into the peace and the triumph of Paradise! Let me press this
thought especially upon you, my dear young
friends, who are here as the companions,
equal in age, of him who has gone. His
pleasant studies, his eager hopes and earnest plans for further study, to be accomplished perhaps abroad, his pleasures, suc-
cesses, and schemes of life, whatever they
were, are ended now. So far as the earthly
life is concerned, the consummation of all is
here; in this still form; this eye, whose light
is quenched in darkness! But, oh! how
precious, beyond compare, to those who
loved him—how precious to himself beyond
all words, beyond all thought—that unob-
trusive faith in Christ he felt and showed;

that sweet submission to all God's will, which made his other graces grander, and which was never so clearly shown as in the hour of parting life!

But, beside this, there are two or three thoughts which seem specially fitting to this occasion. The first is: of the infinite and inexhaustible plentitude of that Divine power that can dispense with even such instruments as these, so costly and so admirable,—with the cultured minds and the consecrated wills that seem precisely adapted to its use—and still can work out, without their aid, the perfect designs of God's wisdom and love.

The experience here presented is not a new one. It is as old as the preaching of Christianity in the world ; as old, one might almost say, as the history of man. Stephen died, full of faith and Christian power, leading, with saintly and shining face, the long procession of Christian martyrs ; looking up into Heaven, and seeing the Son of Man standing to welcome him at the right hand

of God ; his body crushed, life beaten from
it, beneath the furious storm of stones, at
just the crisis when most of all that life to
man's eyes appeared indispensable, to the
church which was so weak, and the world,
whose whole hope was bound up in that
church. But God's design to publish the
Gospel, and to make the empires subject to
his Son, was not arrested by the death of
even this eminent servant. Nay, He made
that death, in its seeming so disastrous, a
means of the progress of His august plan ;
so affecting by it the heart of a bystander,
who was consenting to it, that it is hardly
too much to say, with those of old, that, "if
Stephen had not prayed, the church had not
possessed its Paul," and that we still catch
the echoes of his words whose face appeared
as the face of an angel, through the argument and imagery and the mighty appeals
of the Pauline Epistles.

So in every great movement which Christendom has since seen. So in our own Revolutionary struggle. Nathan Hale dies : the

accomplished student, the stimulating teacher, the affectionate, earnest, exemplary Christian, the soldier whose career was full of promise: he dies ignominiously, in this city of New York, surrendering his life in the cause of his country, and only regretting in the hour of his death that he has but one life to devote to that country. But the Cause is not thwarted; it is not even checked. Warren dies: the pure patriot, the far-sighted statesman, the orator able to electrify and persuade men, the soldier undaunted by any danger, the man without fear and without reproach: and it seems for the time as if the bullet that has blasted his life, and sealed forever his eloquent lips, has fatally shattered the hopes of the country, and stricken the movement represented by him with remediless disaster. But still the great Cause marches on; and the struggle for National Freedom and Union, so early baptized with the blood of its best and noblest champions, is brought at last to a triumphant issue.

And so to-day. This scene is one of how many like scenes, occurring throughout our loyal land! The young, the brave, the charming and the cherished, bright minds, swift wills, and gallant hearts : oh, in how many scattered church-yards, within the year, have such been laid for the last sleep! How many hearts have ached and bled, like these before me, while over the coffins of those they loved they have repeated the sad words : " Died in the field!" " Died in the camp!" " Died at the war!" Over how many churches and villages have tidings of these deaths spread a thick gloom! But shall we therefore be despondent, because the young are dying first? because the strong, who should have borne out others to their burial, are carried themselves in such vast numbers, blanched by the fever or drenched in blood, to be laid down, before their time, for the long rest? No : rather let us the more adore that Power Unsearchable which never is dependent for its success on human instruments ; which is not limited by our economies; which makes the absolute final success consistent with all this lavish expenditure of even the costliest, choicest means; and which works on its wondrous way, to the perfect realization of God's designs, in spite of all combined resistance; unharmed by those who would arrest, unhindered by any defect or failure of force or life in those who would assist it!

I know hardly another point from which I get so grand a view of that eternal and sovereign might which is our God's—of that transcendent power which, as joined with justice and an absolute goodness, is the safeguard of the universe, the object of constant angelic praise, and the prime condition of all our hopes—as comes to me here! Not when I think of the forces and laws that gird and guide this whirling earth, of the mountains God has reared, or the oceans whose beds His hands have scooped, or of the whole material universe—not standing in space on pillars of adamant, but suspended forever on the word of His power! but

when I reflect how untroubled are His plans
by what to us looks most disastrous! how
He does not care to protect by His providence what we count most important to His
purpose! and how with absolute steadiness
of accomplishment His plans move on, though
hundreds and thousands of those who would
perform them are fainting by the way! How
vast the resources, which even such a loss
and waste as here appears, in no wise lessens!
How unspeakable the energy which can dispense with these noble auxiliaries, and be no
whit less certain of the result!

And another thought as natural to the
occasion, and which seems irresistibly impressed upon my heart as I stand here to-
day, is that of *the greatness and glory of the
Future, for this our Nation, which is to be
wrought out for it at last through all this sacrifice, suffering, death!*

I know there are other points, not a few,
from which the same great thought is suggested. As we look back to the long, slow
series of centuries through which this con-

tinent remained hidden so perfectly from the eyes of the world; as we see how promptly it was brought to the light when the era of advancing Reformation had been reached, and forces were developed and at work within Christendom, adapted, as transferred here, to make it a kingdom of God and of his Son; as we notice what care and pains God took to people it from the start with representatives of the best religious culture the world had reached; and how he has trained, and disciplined, and enriched this people ever since, and has made of the early scattered colonies a great Christian Nation, whose unity may be threatened but cannot be broken, and whose influence must extend more widely, through commerce and literature, laws and arts, the missions of the Cross and the example of Liberty, with every year; nay, as we look upon the country itself, so apt for tillage, so wealthy with metallic and mineral treasures, laced and bound inextricably together by such ranges of mountains and such vast rivers, and so poised

and set on the crest of the earth that its
influence strikes almost of necessity across
both oceans, around the world :—it is impossible *not* to feel that He who has pur-
posed and has conducted thus far this
wonderful history, and has fashioned and
framed this unequaled arena for a grand
Christian Nation, intends to fulfill His own
prophecies concerning it! intends to make
it a Nation to His praise ; and to give it at
home such a Christian development, and to
give it abroad such a reach and sweep of
Christian influence, as no other nation, nor
this itself, has yet approached ; as almost
none has ever conceived !—Undoubtedly, my
Brethren, this is to be.   It is ours to believe
it ; and on the sure and steadfast pillars of
this great hope, of this certain expectation,
to take hold with strong faith whensoever
we are timid concerning our Nation, that
there may come new strength to our souls,
a new ardor and energy to all our exertions.
The great visions of the Fathers are here to
be fulfilled.   The thunderous discords now

shattering the air, are to be hushed by-and-
by ; giving place to " hallelujahs and harping
symphonies." And an empire is at last to be
here, one, free, Christian, mighty, for the fur-
therance of the reign of Messiah in the world.

But nowhere, as I said, does this great
thought come to me so vividly, nowhere else
is the certainty of this sublime Future so
impressed upon my heart, as when I stand
in a scene like this, and remember that this
is but one of multitudes, occurring simulta-
neously, occurring continuously, in these
late months, in city and village, from the
Eastern slopes to the shores of the Pacific!
This discipline of our suffering—how sud-
denly it has come! How stern it is ; and
how wide-reaching! Ah, think how many
are being trained by it! Not the wounded
or sickening soldier alone ; not he only
who lies in his stiffening garments upon the
torn and trampled battle-ground, in the
furrowed ridges which the cannon have
ploughed, or he who lies down, as did our
friend, in the lonely tent afar from home,

20*

where no domestic care watches over him,
and no dear face of parent or friend is near
to cheer ; but they, as well, who from farm-
house or mansion look out for his coming
who shall no more return to them : they
who watch with faint hearts for the letter
or the message that does not reach them till
too late : fathers, mothers, sisters, brothers,
whose hearts are shaken by every report of
the distant artillery that flies across the
reverberating wires, whose souls are pierced
with shafts of pain by every bullet that
strikes the ranks in which their dear ones
are arrayed :—all *these* are the sufferers
whom this discipline touches! Shall there
not be an outcome, precious and grand, to
the Nation which God has so planted and
watched, from this vast pain? Shall not the
people that was growing too fierce, ambi-
tious, and sensual, through its constant suc-
cesses, be taught and trained for a far
nobler errand by this sharp sorrow that
searches now, with almost omnipresent probe,
its inmost heart?

Certainly, my Brethren, certainly, it shall be! Even according to our human economies, by the price that is paid may be usually measured the good that is gained. By the labor of the hands, and the active exertion of brain and will, we buy outward wealth; or even, it may be, mental accomplishments. By love, alone, do we gain love, that grander good. Through nothing less than long endurance do we achieve victorious character. By suffering, only, are we changed, through God's grace, into the likeness of Him, our Lord, who, innocent as He was, was the chiefest of sufferers; that having been partakers of His patience on earth, we may be partakers of His triumph on high. The very Church of Christ is purchased, with His own blood. And so I know that God has great and precious things reserved in His purpose for us as a people, to be wrought out in us, and then wrought out for us, through this immense but remedial pain! If it were only material prosperity that He had reserved for us—of mountains tunneled and valleys bridged, of mines explored, and great energies subjugated, of rivers echoing to the tramp of the wheel, and cities shining on the marge of the lakes, and villages strung like glittering pearls on the threads of the railways, of homes being multiplied, and universities rising, and an affluent commerce, encompassing the globe, —then all this might be accomplished, with His aid, through foresight and fortitude, an inventive, intrepid, and masterful sagacity ; and to these alone He would then train us. But when I think of all these forms, shrouded in pale or bloody death—of all these hearts wrung with an anguish unfelt before, in our late history,—of all those happy Christian homes, wherein the very tenderness of love is now the occasion of fear and pain that pass all words—I know that it is not *such* a prosperity, alone, that awaits us! An argument comes for our ultimate unity, and Christian supremacy, from the very severity of this present sorrow. It must be that we are to buy redemption from long iniquities, by these fierce pangs, this bloody sweat. And never does the vast and magnificent temple of American Liberty, as it is to be in the centuries to come, arise before me in such an august and radiant beauty, so lovely, so majestic, so capacious, so enduring, as when I remember that its great columns are now being planted, and its ascending pillars set, in all these thousands of Christian graves!

The last thought I have to suggest is this: What a light is cast by the death of one like him before us, in the early prime and vigor of life, with every power just springing upward to its maturity—what a light is cast on the *offices of Heaven;* on the *nature of the Life* that shall there open to us ; as full of great works, giving scope illimitable to each bright faculty, to each high power, that stirs within us!—If only the infant, the young child, died, we should think of Heaven as a home of kindness, a sphere of culture, a nursery only for the infantile mind. If only the aged were to die

—falling like shocks of corn fully ripe in their season, rounding with death a life long protracted, and the energy of whose powers was beginning to fail—we should then think of Heaven only as a scene of reward and repose; of rest after toil; of long tranquillity after long service. But when the young and strong are taken, they whose faculties seemed to prophesy large development, and whose elastic and untired spirit was even then, with the keenest vitality, impelling them forward to exertion and activity—we know that Heaven is something other than either a shelter and school for babes, or a home of quiet repose for the aged. Our thoughts run on instinctively to its scenes, and anticipate amid them opportunities and offices such as shall meet the utmost demands of the young and fresh spirit, inspired with desires for knowledge and wisdom, capable of and eager for a various, wide-ranging, and beneficent use of the force God has given it. And so there come to us new and more just conceptions, I think, of the Life Everlasting.

It is not song, only, that shall occupy us there; but a vast yet unfatiguing service, for God and for the Universe; a service transformed into a nobler than any audible praise by the spirit of Love that pervades and transfigures it! No inlet to pleasure, no capacity for it, but shall be more than satisfied there! No pure sensibility, no delicate taste, no thirst for affection, no energy of will, no finest or lordliest power of the soul, but shall find there its most perfect exhibition, its most exuberant joy and use! And though we cannot prefigure precisely the work to be done there, or the embassies of love on which they shall forever go forth who are lifted from the earth to those sublime heights, we know, as we stand beside a coffin like this, and think of him who was with us so lately, and who henceforth is with the Master, that not vacant or barren is that Immortality which to him hath been opened; that full, on the other hand, is it forever of vivacity and variety, of stimulation and success, of sympathy and activity, of usefulness and reward! The stream has passed beyond the point where our eyes follow it; but we know, as certainly as we know that God lives, that it flows on still, with only a swifter and mightier current. The star has faded from our sight; but only because its lustre is completed in the perfect effulgence of the Heavenly Day!

Let me congratulate you then, my Friends, the parents of him who sleeps before us, that he has been counted worthy by Christ to arise to all this, which our thoughts cannot compass; of which the very prophetic vision can tell our darkened minds so little! We are not here to offer comfort, alone; although of that how many are the sources! But we are here rather to recognize with you, with joy of heart, God's tokens of love which have come to you with this sorrow; in even its circumstances, as well as in itself. We thank Him, with you, that the voice of

Christian adoration and praise was heard
in the tent where your son passed on, alone
but unalarmed, through the shadow of Death.
We thank God, with you, that he was permitted to send to you, and you to receive,
his last messages of remembrance and of
filial affection ; and that you have been
permitted to bring him, unmarred of decay,
in the still and solemn beauty of death, to
this familiar house and altar, and with these
appropriate funeral rites to close the coffin
above the dear dust ! But more than for
all things else, we thank God, and with you
offer to Him our praise, that He has opened
to this your son those gates of peace through
which have passed Apostles' feet, the Martyrs', and the Saints', and Christ the Lord's !
that he, henceforth, from all trial and pain is
free forever ! Not in the European schools
shall he pursue his further studies, but in
that "better country, even an heavenly,"
where Paul shall teach, and Gabriel shall
hear, the wonders of God's love in man's
Redemption. He would have been promoted,

21

if he had lived, to higher rank in the National service. But Christ hath called him— He who in righteousness doth judge and make war, upon whose head are many crowns, and who hath on His vesture and on His thigh a name written, King of Kings, and Lord of Lords—He hath called him to nobler office, in a how far sublimer warfare! Look up, then, and not down; to Paradise on high, and not to the grave; and know that every day and hour, if we are faithful, but brings us nearer to that same wonder, that ecstasy and mystery, of vision and of victory, which he hath reached! Ah! when we shall at last attain it, and join again the souls, so many and so beloved, who have gone on to it before us, what words or harps shall be sufficient to speak to God or tell to Saints our perfect praise!

www.ingramcontent.com/pod-product-compliance
Lightning Source LLC
Chambersburg PA
CBHW020106030726
47498CB00006B/1973